If lent or lost please return to;

MARY KEEGAN, Price

SO-AXL-040

number 1

0'30

RECEIVED 21 SEP 1970

Second hand books in English

THE SPANISH GARDENER

Also by A. J. Cronin and available in the NEL series

THE CITADEL
THE STARS LOOK DOWN
HATTER'S CASTLE
SHANNON'S WAY
THE KEYS OF THE KINGDOM
A SONG OF SIXPENCE

The Spanish Gardener

A. J. Cronin

HIBERNIAN BOOKS
MONTSENY 17 BARCELONA
93 217 47 96
NO EXCHANGE BOOK

NEL

THE NEW ENGLISH LIBRARY

First published in Great Britain by Victor Gollancz Ltd, in 1950
Second impression April 1958
Third impression August 1960
Fourth impression January 1963
Copyright 1950 by A. J. Cronin

*

First published as a Four Square Edition September 1965
Reprinted August 1967
Reissued in this NEL edition March 1968

*

Conditions of Sale: This book is sold subject to the condition that it shall not, by way of trade or otherwise, be lent, re-sold, hired out, or otherwise circulated without the publisher's prior consent in any form of binding or cover other than that in which it is published and without a similar condition including this condition being imposed on the subsequent purchaser.

NEL Books are published by The New English Library Limited from Barnard's Inn, Holborn, London, E.C.1. Made and printed in Great Britain by Hunt Barnard & Co., Ltd., Aylesbury, Bucks.

45000080 X

THE SPANISH GARDENER

ONE

THE OVERNIGHT JOURNEY from Paris had been unusually wearisome. An exasperating delay at the junction of Port Bou on the Spanish frontier had made them forty minutes late and, because of a dilatory porter, they had missed the morning connection at Barcelona. Now, towards five o'clock in the afternoon as they bounced and rattled to their destination on the light railway of the Costa Brava, they were tired and travel-stained. The shortcomings of men, or of machines, always irked the Consul and his mood was not propitious. Seated erect in his corner, he frowned with concern at his little son who, bundled up on the wooden seat opposite, in the long, littered coach redolent of dust, garlic and stale country odours, had been stealing glances of affectionate timidity towards him. And for the third time in the past hour, he inquired:

"You are all right, Nicholas?"

"Quite all right, Father."

The curvetting engine, in final indignity, threw them round a vertiginous curve and, with a shrill whistle, drew into the deserted station of San Jorge. Leaving the rug and the two valises, the Consul took Nicholas's hand and stepped to the platform, a deserted strip inch-deep in red dust, fringed by a string of palmettos so ravaged by the wind they drooped like spavined horses. At first, with a darkening of his brow, he thought they had not been met, then his eye cleared. A young man in a neat linen suit, rather shrunk by washing, a bow tie and yellow straw hat, stood at the entrance beside a grey automobile with a miniature American flag on the radiator cap, and at the sight of the two passengers he hurried nervously forward, followed by the driver.

"Mr. Harrington Brande? Very happy to see you, sir. We missed you on the morning train. I'm Alvin Burton, from the

7

office." He turned to the chauffeur, a dark, thickly built Spaniard wearing a black alpaca jacket, denim trousers and sharp-pointed tan shoes. "Will you get the luggage, please, Garcia?"

The open car, Brande noted with some alleviation of his irritation, was a respectable Pierce-Arrow, with well-polished brass, pipe-clayed tyres, and freshly laundered white covers on the upholstery. While the bags were being brought he stood aside, a tall, heavy figure, with a slight, distinguished stoop, his long, sallow face, deeply furrowed at the nostrils, wearing that air of noncommittal dignity which he reserved for his subordinates.

"I do hope you'll be comfortable at the residence, sir," Alvin was saying. "Mr. Tenney took his servants with him. But I've done my best to engage a good couple. Garcia, the chauffeur-butler"—he lowered his voice—"has exceptional testimonials . . . and Magdalena, his wife, is an excellent cook."

Harrington Brande inclined his head.

"Are we ready?"

"Yes, indeed, sir," Alvin exclaimed, rather breathlessly.

They got into the car. As they drove off the new Consul let his gaze roam over the town, still clasping protectively, under cover of the rug, the thin, damp fingers of his son. It was not, perhaps, he reflected, with a gleam of hope, so detestable a place as he had feared. The air was pure, the curving waterfront, along which they glided in the fading February sunshine, had a fringe of clean sand, and between the electric light standards the esplanade was planted, though somewhat raggedly, with flowering acacias. In the Plaza a fountain played amongst the scarlet blossoms of ponciana shrubs, the peeling gilt of a bandstand glittered beyond the black figures of old men reading *La Gaceta*, an antique bus discharged its passengers, a pleasant sense of life prevailed. Opposite the inevitable pink stucco church with twin cupolas like upturned breasts, its central belfry set with coloured tiles and surmounted by a tarnished cross, there were one or two

8

moderate shops, a café, El Chantaco, with a blue-striped awning, which seemed tolerable, and further down the Calle, beside the harbour, a solid commercial block in which, Burton now murmured, was situated the office of the Consulate.

But no, near at hand, he could not but observe that the docks, upon which his work must largely centre, bore a listless and dejected aspect—they looked half-dead, in fact; he guessed that nothing much would stir there but a sluggish trade in hides, fertiliser, cork bark, olive oil and Tarragona vinegar. Only two fishing scows lay at the jetty, and a rusted coastal steamer from which, aided by three donkeys and a primitive pulley, some sailors were languidly discharging barrels. And again the old wave of bitterness swept over him, fixing his expression with a kind of brooding heaviness. Why, oh why, at the age of forty-five, after fifteen years of sedulous devotion to duty in Europe, was he sent to such a dead end, a man of his talent and personality who had long ago earned the right, if only through seniority, to one of the high positions of the service in Paris, Rome or London ? After these last eighteen months, bogged amidst the Normandy marshes at Arville, he had hoped that his next move would bring him his due reward. And then . . . San Jorge . . . worse still, the realisation that Tenney, his predecessor here, and his junior by three years, had been promoted First Consul under Leighton Bailey at Madrid.

"Look, Father, isn't that pretty?"

They had left the town, had climbed a steep, winding, sandy lane between rows of silvery eucalyptus trees, and Nicholas, aroused and interested, was pointing shyly to the view now visible from the summit. A great sweep of Mediterranean sea lay beneath, with a slender lighthouse creamed by white surf upon the rocky promontory of the bay. Further to the north tremendous mountains unveiled their outlines dimly through the blue haze. The air had a fresh tang of salt and aromatic herbs. And just ahead, on the edge of a *barranco* smothered in pearly cistus petals, almost screened from the lane by a

9

high mimosa hedge, stood a rambling, red-tiled villa with the name, Casa Breza, in faded letters upon the pillared entrance.

"You like it?" Alvin Burton turned towards the boy, and from his tone, expectant and a little anxious, Nicholas became aware that this was his new home. He had known many changes in his brief nine years and so had lost something of his capacity to be surprised. Yet this strange old house, with its deserted air and magnificent seclusion, gave promise of unusual attractions. The Consul seemed of similar opinion, for as they ran with a crunching of wheels into the gravel driveway and got out of the car his sharp, appraising glance was gradually mellowed by approval.

Built of the local yellow sandstone, faded now to a delicate amber, the villa was in Moorish style, with a spacious arched portico, and a flat, overhanging roof tiled in a shade of weathered cinnabar. The upstairs windows opened upon a wide balcony, profusely overgrown with wistaria and tangled vines, with lilac and the flaming shoots of biscutella. To the left a cobbled yard, green with moss, gave access to the stables and other outbuildings. The garden lay beyond.

"It's old, of course," Alvin remarked excusingly, watching his chief's face. "And a little out of repair. Also there's no electricity, only gas. But Mr. Tenney always felt he was lucky to have it. There are really no proper living quarters near the office, and we have a long lease here . . . furnished. . . ."

"Yes," said the Consul shortly.

Bracing his shoulders, he strode up the shallow steps of the portico towards the open doorway, where a stout middle-aged woman in a respectable black dress, whom Burton introduced as Magdalena, stood waiting to receive them with a smile.

Inside, the tessellated hall was cool and lofty, the dining-room on one hand, the *salon*, with double doors, upon the other, both apartments furnished in rococo style. A wide staircase in dark walnut spiralled upwards from the rear and, despite his fatigue, the Consul, as one who knew his duty and his rights, ascended heavily, to make an inspection of the

10

upper rooms. There were many more than he and his little son, and perhaps an occasional guest, could utilise, but this was not displeasing to a man whose tastes were cast in a large and superior mould. He liked the sense of space, the inlaid chests and credenzas, the tapestried gilt chairs, tasselled bell-pulls and faded velvet curtains; even the slightly musty odour which pervaded the long corridors fell agreeably upon his nostrils. When his heavy baggage arrived there would be ample room for his books and porcelain, his remarkable collection, gathered in many places over the years, of antique weapons.

When he returned to the vestibule it was evident that he was satisfied, and Alvin's brown eyes glistened with relief. Like a faithful dog, he perked up, expectant of some word of approbation.

"I trust everything's in order, sir. There's not been much time since Mr. Tenney left. I've done my best."

"Of course," the Consul replied suavely, yet with his most cryptic air. He knew better than to begin his régime with indiscriminate praise of his assistant. Nothing so easily impaired strict discipline, nor fostered more quickly the disaster of familiarity. Besides, he had already decided that this raw, nervous young man, in the tight-fitting suit—burst, indeed, in one place, at the armpit—was socially impossible, best kept at a distance. And as Alvin hung on, turning his straw hat in his hands, as if hoping to be asked to stay a little, for a glass of sherry perhaps, Brande civilly, yet firmly, conducted him towards the door.

"I shall see you at the office to-morrow, then, Mr. Burton."

"Very good, sir."

"You are always there at nine sharp."

"Oh, of course." Rather red above the collar, Alvin prepared to take his leave, but hesitated on the front steps and, in a manner which made Nicholas look appealingly at his father, stammered: "May I express the hope, sir, that you will honour Mrs. Burton and myself by a visit to our apart-

11

ment in the Calle Estrada. It's a small place, but we've tried to make it a little bit of the good old U.S.A."

The Consul replied with perfect politeness, but when Alvin had gone his lip curled. No one could question his loyalty to his country, yet was he not now a complete cosmopolitan, refined and polished by European culture, a citizen of the world, in fact? No wonder Alvin's naïve phrase made him smile.

It was now seven o'clock and, with admirable anticipation of his master's wishes, Garcia announced that the dinner was served. Two places had been laid in the large dining-room and, seating themselves at either end of the long, carved refectory table, with a sconce of lighted candles between, father and son began the first meal in their new home.

For the most part, occupied by his own thoughts and deeply solicitous of Nicholas's fatigue, the Consul kept silent. But the excellence of the cooking and the service, the pleasing atmosphere of the dim, cool, lofty room, gradually soothed his spirit, and erased the manifold irritations which had tried him so sorely during the day. With his heavy, brooding eyes he followed the movement of the butler, and finally he raised the barrier of his reserve.

"Your name is Garcia, I understand?"

"Yes, señor."

"You have always been in San Jorge?"

Garcia straightened himself without a movement of his impassive face. The flicker of the candle flames was reflected for an instant at the back of his expressionless eyes.

"No, señor. I have been in much larger cities. And always with the best people. My previous situation was with the de Aostas in Madrid."

"You mean the Marquesa de Aosta?"

"A branch of that family, señor."

Harrington Brande nodded in recognition of the fact. He would have been the first to resent the imputation that he was a snob. Nevertheless, he was strongly conscious of the social order, and it did not displease him that this silent personage

12

who now served him should bear, so to speak, an aristocratic recommendation.

"Tell the cook I will see her in the morning. My son is somewhat delicate and will require a special diet." When the man bowed and noiselessly departed he remarked to Nicholas, with satisfaction, "He seems a superior fellow."

The word 'superior,' whether he applied it to a horse, a servant, or to his intimate friend, Professor Halevy of Paris, was the Consul's most-favoured expression of approbation. Yet for once Nicholas could not share his father's feelings. Indeed, the butler had produced in him, from the moment of his first sidelong glance, a sensation curiously disagreeable which he could not well explain.

After the Consul had finished his coffee he looked significantly at his gold repeater watch. However, Nicholas, upon whom the exciting strangeness of the place was already working like a ferment, pleaded most eagerly that they might take a turn in the garden before he went upstairs, and his father indulgently consented.

Outside, with a coat wrapped about his thin shoulders to protect him from any chance of chill, the little boy drew in deep breaths of the soft, spicy air which seemed to sweep in from infinity, submerging all consciousness of time and space. Although his head still rang with the tumult of the journey, he felt the peace of the falling evening upon him and upon the garden. It was larger, oh, much larger, than he had expected, and gloriously rank. A path led downwards from the portico under three pergolas bent beneath great braids of roses, flanked on either side by a broad herbaceous border, wild with primulas and great white peonies. To the left there stood a thicket of myrtle and oleanders, pink and white, already in full-scented flower. Upon the other hand, the garden opened to a kind of meadow, which might once have been a lawn, bearing two lovely trees, a wide catalpa and a tamarisk, then, beyond a low boundary wall and a wooden tool-shed, there lay a rocky heath, studded with white boulders, spiny cacti, and tufts of purple azalea. Behind, clumps of laurel masked

13

the stables and domestic quarters, while in front the land fell, not steeply, to some woods of stunted cedar, thence to the level of the shore.

Standing beside his father, viewing all this beauty, intoxicated by the scents of earth and springing growth, Nicholas was conscious suddenly of a presentiment, a surging confidence, never before experienced in any of their previous abodes, that he could—ah, no, that he would be happy here. From below there came the wild yet gentle sighing of the surf. An access of joy made him shut his eyes lest tears should flow from them. He felt his chest rising in deep, slow breaths of glad anticipation.

"Isn't it nice, Father?" he murmured, to prolong the moment.

Despite himself, the Consul smiled, that rare smile which only Nicholas could evoke. He too was not indifferent to the charm of the garden and, with his eyes upon the tangled oleander bushes and the rangy mimosa hedge which Tenney had 'let go,' his thoughts ran, a little grandly, to a policy of reclamation, of fresh planting, landscaping and topiary work.

"It *could* be nice," he agreed indulgently. "We must have a gardener. I shall see about it to-morrow."

As they went back to the house he gazed tenderly at his son, wondering, hopefully, if this garden, this pure, strong air, sweeping from the Sierras and the sea, might not bring health to him.

On the first floor he had chosen for Nicholas and himself two adjoining front bedrooms connected by a curtained doorway through which he would be available if his son should call him in the night. He himself was a light sleeper who suffered severely from insomnia. Yet his ever-watchful and protective love had always demanded that he should be close at hand during these nocturnal hours when, so frequently, distressing nightmares caused Nicholas to start into palpitating wakefulness, his heart beating frantically, his forehead bathed in a cold sweat of dread. This was a feature

14

of the child's invalidism which caused the Consul most concern.

Upstairs, the valises were already unpacked and it was not long before Nicholas had undressed and washed himself, swallowed through a glass tube the iron tonic which Professor Halevy had prescribed for him, and brushed his teeth. Then in a fresh nightshirt he knelt at his father's side to say his prayers. Despite the sophistication that his long sojourn in Europe had given him, Harrington Brande was still—he gravely admitted it—a religious man. He might smile a little at his New England ancestors, yet their Puritan spirit remained strong within him. He listened with bowed head, his hand upon his dear son's shoulder, and at the end he himself added a special petition that the Almighty might protect them both and bless their sojourn now beginning in this new habitation. Then he paused and in a low and muffled voice, in words which seemed wrenched from the centre of his being, he added:

"We ask God's mercy for all transgressors . . . and in particular, dear child . . . we ask it for your mother."

A moment later Nicholas was in the big Cordova bed, its end-piece covered in stamped yellow leather and edged with heavy brass studs. Yet still the Consul lingered, glancing with a kind of self-conscious hesitation at the slight figure lost, almost, under the great brocaded counterpane.

"Of course, dear boy . . . you are too tired for our reading to-night."

Nicholas, indeed, was dizzy from fatigue, and his eyelids, violet-shadowed in his small, pale face, were drooping as though drugged with sleep. Yet he knew how much store his father set by this final chapter of their evening ritual and, summoning a smile, he protested that he was still quite wide awake.

Again the Consul hesitated, but only for a moment, before yielding to the inclination which his affection, his passion for his beloved child, made him loath to forego. Entering his own room, he returned speedily with a heavy bound volume of

15

Akerman's *Book of Ornithology*, seated himself beside the soft Cordova bed, and put on his horn-rimmed glasses.

"You remember, Nicholas, that on our last evening at Arville we were discussing the birds of South Africa—a most interesting subject. We shall not take much to-night, just enough to keep ourselves in touch. Ah, here we are." He had turned the pages until he found the place and now, clearing his throat, he began to read:

"The ostrich, genus *Struthio*, characterised by the possession of two toes and the absence of keel on the breast bone, is the largest living bird. The male may be nearly seven feet high and weigh as much as three hundred pounds. Ranging the sandy plains and open country, it is fleet of foot and when brought to bay can be extremely fierce. The birds are immensely vain of their feathers, and the male especially displays great solicitude for its young. . . ."

TWO

NEXT MORNING THE Consul rose early and left punctually for his office. Nicholas, unfortunately, had passed an unquiet night in which, through the torpor which bound him, the events of the journey, the grinding of engine wheels, the sound of the surf and, for some absurd reason, the dark, impassive figure of the butler were inextricably mingled. His temperature showed normal, but his father seemed to detect a lingering flush of excitement upon his cheeks, and insisted that the boy remain in bed, promising, however, to return at noon to see if he might get up for lunch.

It was a disappointment for Nicholas, who wished he might at least have lain outside in that lovely garden. But he was an obedient child, well versed by now in his own physical deficiencies, in the regular routine of thermometer-reading and pulse-checking prescribed by Professor Halevy and, in a

16

queer, prim way, gratefully expectant of the solicitude which his father constantly bestowed upon him.

Magdalena brought up his breakfast, rather breathless from her ascent of the stairs, but quite friendly, her black eyes almost hidden by the creases in her plump brown cheeks. A white scarf wrapped about her head and two metal rings dangling from her ears gave her an interesting gipsy look. Thanks to his father's tutoring, Nicholas spoke creditable Spanish—he had, indeed, a precocious knowledge of French and Italian besides—but Magdalena's rapid chatter was some kind of dialect, Catalan he thought, and they could not understand each other very well. As she stood there, with hands on her hips, he detected a frank peasant curiosity in her gaze and, in response, he dramatised himself a little, blinking his long eyelashes and swallowing his breath so that he could break it in his stomach with an alarming rumble. At this she laughed shortly, shook her head, and went away.

The breakfast was his usual, and quite nice: a lightly boiled egg, crisp rusks and comb honey, a glass of boiled goat's milk; obviously his father had been giving orders in the kitchen. Nicholas ate the food slowly, using his experience to avoid putting crumbs on the sheet. Then he hopped out and brought over the woolly hound which, with four short legs planted on the dressing table, had silently and faithfully awaited his attentions. Nicholas knew, of course, that he could not possess a live dog; the Consul, himself no dog-lover, had logically explained how this was precluded by the difficulties and uncertainties of their too mobile existence, so the child had made the best of this small stuffed substitute. This morning, however, he was scarcely in the mood for one of those long conversations which so often beguiled, for both of them, the tedious hours. Nor could he bring himself to glance, more than perfunctorily, at the lesson books which his father had placed, convenient to his hand, on the bedside table. No, he was too highly keyed by the novelty of these still unexplored surroundings and, while a bright square of sunlight slid warmly across the striped maroon wallpaper, stamped with strange arabesques, which fancy might make still stranger, he lay on his back, listening, as it were, to the silent heart-beat of the house.

Yet the beat was not altogether silent. Sounds came from downstairs, disturbing sounds, as of an argument, high words, followed by the banging of what Nicholas guessed to be the kitchen door. Then came the low undertone of whispering, footsteps in the dining-room below, unhurried tidying-up movements, an ascending whiff of strong tobacco. Construing all this, somewhat rigidly, Nicholas was taken aback, quite startled in fact, by the sudden quiet opening of his door. He turned and there, gazing at him with a confidential air, was Garcia.

Unaccountably, the blood rushed to the little boy's cheeks. That queer distrust of the butler which he had felt on the previous evening, as though from the outset he sensed in him an enemy, returned with redoubled force at this unexpected materialisation.

"Shall I take your tray?" Garcia spoke with exaggerated deference, in his usual insinuating manner, yet, as if to give that the lie, he kept his cigarette burning between his nicotined fingers.

"Please . . . thank you." Nicholas answered in a small, unsteady voice.

The man did not move but showed his teeth in what, but for the general immobility of his features, might have been a smile.

"Don't mind me," he said softly. "I am well used to children. In one place there were seven. The little girl used to sit upon my knee. Before she died."

Nicholas took a quick breath. The butler drew deeply, absently, upon his brown cigarette, yet never removed his eyes from the small boy's face.

"One day I will tell you about her. It would make an interesting talk for us. I've seen many things. Sad and horrible things. Unbelievable things. The world is full of idiots. Nothing matters to me, absolutely nothing."

18

"What do you mean?" Nicholas gasped.

Garcia shrugged indifferently.

"You will see. I have been a soldier. An officer. I have seen men flogged, tortured, and shot. But we will speak of that another time. Tell me. Where is your mother?"

Nicholas turned pale. The question, thrown casually, yet with a hidden insolence, pierced anew the deepest, the most secret, scar in his shrinking soul. For an instant of panic he thought of answering, 'She is dead.' Had not his father insisted often, with melancholy gravity, that she must now, indeed, be considered as dead to both of them? And only that evening Christian prayer for her forgiveness saved her from an oblivion equal to the grave. Yet an instinct within him repudiated the lie, less from a natural innocence than from the strange precognition that if he lied to this man his defences would, once and for all, be swept away. He would be lost.

"She is in America," he stammered.

"Ah!" Garcia exclaimed. "A wonderful country. But why not here?"

With a trembling of his chin which made his lips and delicate nostrils quiver, and the skin of his forehead contract, Nicholas brought out the words:

"Mother doesn't live with us any more."

Garcia parted his thin wide lips in a silent laugh.

"So she is nothing to us. She lives apart. But we cannot escape from people that way." He broke off, listening, as measured footsteps sounded on the steps of the portico. There was a pause then; without change of manner, yet perhaps with a faint shade of caution, he nodded. "Your father has come back. You must not tell him of our interesting conversation. Now we have a secret, you and I. Do not forget that, little innocent."

He advanced to the bed and, using only one hand, expertly hoisted up the tray; then, with a half-bow, tinged with that same servile mockery, he turned and went out of the room.

Nicholas lay there, his brow still contracted, filled with

19

perplexity and confusion. He felt discouraged, strangely empty, and only the prompt appearance of his father prevented him from bursting into tears.

The Consul was in good spirits, evidently not displeased with his morning's work and, after a brief inspection, he bade Nicholas get up. Seated on the end of the bed while the boy dressed, he proved more than usually discursive. The office was better than he had expected, small yet quite modern, and situated on the Marina, where the sea breezes would be agreeable in summer. Besides Alvin Burton, there were two Spanish clerks on the staff. He had found the equipment in sound condition except for a faulty typewriter which could be repaired, and a broken mimeograph machine which he had immediately ordered to be replaced.

"And now," the Consul went on with continuing liveliness, "you may be interested that I have found you a gardener. He's outside, in the yard. Come along and take a look at him."

They went downstairs, Nicholas walking sedately at his father's side.

Outside, waiting at the back entrance, in an attitude of respectful attention, was a tall, well-proportioned youth of nineteen years, with open features and sloe-dark, gentle eyes. His eyebrows were strongly marked, his hair sprouted black and bushy, and upon his upper lip there lay already an immature, pathetic shadow. It was a simple face and could have been handsome, in spite of its saffron colouring, but for the soft, full mouth, which hung a little open. The young man wore his best suit, a shoddy but well-brushed serge, the jacket cut very short, Catalan fashion, and the trousers billowing slightly at the turn-up, covering the broken shoes. In his large brown hands he held a round, flat hat.

"Well, here you are, my lad," said the Consul with agreeable briskness. "What did you say was your name?"

"José, *señor* . . . José Santero."

"And you are an expert gardener?"

José smiled, deprecatingly, showing beautiful white teeth.

20

It was a warm, natural smile, and so infectious it made Nicholas want to smile back.

"I know how to dig, and hoe, and care for the soil, *señor*. I can prune and plant. I am very willing. But I am not so expert."

"I understood you had experience," Brande remarked somewhat impatiently.

"Oh, yes, *señor*," José answered quickly. "For three years I worked in the Montaro vineyards. But now there is much unemployment in the hills."

"You have testimonials?"

With a faintly lost air, smiling yet doubtful, José's gaze passed from the Consul and came to rest upon the little boy.

"We do not trouble about such things, *señor*. If you ask Diego Borgano, at Montara, I think he would speak well of me."

There was a pause. Nicholas gazed up anxiously at his father who, biting his lip, was plainly debating this aspect of the matter, and he had strongly to suppress an impulse, which he knew would only prejudice José's case, to beg his father to engage this gardener who was so young, so friendly, and so nice.

The sound of the luncheon gong hastened the Consul's decision. After all, they had given the fellow a good character at the Exchange. He spoke brusquely.

"I shall expect you to work hard, you know. The pay is thirty pesetas a week. Do you agree?"

"I do not quarrel with the *señor's* wishes," José answered soberly.

"Very good," said Harrington Brande. "Be here at eight o'clock to-morrow and I'll show you what I want done. Come along, dear boy."

He took his son's arm and moved off. As Nicholas went towards the house he had a warm picture of the Spanish youth standing there, gentle and humble, yet strangely proud in his poor Sunday clothes, holding the ridiculous hard hat in his fine brown hands. Irresistibly, as he followed his father up

21

the veranda steps, he looked back over his shoulder and smiled. José's white teeth flashed in an answering smile and to the little boy's joy he waved his arm in gay acknowledgment. Something in that gesture went straight to the child's heart . . . he kept thinking of it during lunch, and afterwards too, with little inward chuckles of delight.

THREE

A PLACE HAD BEEN made for Nicholas in the shelter of the oleanders, a kind of arbour formed by their flowering, overhanging branches, and here, following the schedule laid down by his father, he spent most of his time between lunch and tea, reclining on a chaise-longue, absorbing the briny ozone, and perusing the pages of a book, which must necessarily be profitable, since the Consul himself had selected it.

This afternoon, however, the child's eyes strayed frequently, though secretly, from the printed page, towards the figure of the new gardener working in the overgrown border beneath the catalpa tree. For two days now Nicholas had longed to speak to him, but no opportunity had presented itself and he was, of course, too shy to make one. But now, from José's rate of progress, as he dug steadily with his *azada* along the border, cleaning out the weeds and breaking up the soil, the boy could see that very soon the other would be beside him, and his heart began to beat a little faster at the prospect, for he had from the beginning felt a current of sympathetic understanding—he could not more fully explain it—flowing, flowing gently between the Spanish youth and himself. Perhaps he was wrong. It might be that José was like Garcia, a person who flattered only to deceive, yet he could not bring himself even to entertain such an idea; the disappointment would be more than he could bear.

At last the gardener reached the arbour and, straightening himself, leaned his elbows on the long spade handle, smiled

22

directly at Nicholas. The little boy knew that he must speak first, yet he could think of nothing to say and, when he did, for a long awkward moment the words stuck in his throat.

"You have been working very hard," he stammered, finally, with his usual nervous flush.

"No, no." José's smile widened, and he shrugged his sun-burned shoulders. His torso was bare, and the tight-belted cotton trousers, which he wore with rope-soled *espadrilles*, showed the clean, strong lines of his graceful limbs. His skin, smooth and golden, had a warm, living texture from the supple play of muscles underneath. Despite his exertions, his breath came quietly. After a short pause he added naïvely: "You do not work?"

"I do these." With a more vivid colour, Nicholas indicated his books lying on the wicker table beside him.

"Ah, yes." José nodded gravely, as though in acknowledgment of a superior intelligence. "I think you are very clever."

"Oh, no," protested Nicholas with a heightening of his blush. "But I have to rest a good deal and that is why I read."

"You are sick just now?" José suggested.

"I always have a little fever," Nicholas consciously explained. "I am not strong."

José's gentle smile deepened.

"Perhaps if you worked like me you would be strong." He held out his hand. "Come. I have finished digging and am going to plant. You shall help me."

Nicholas was speechless with delight—he hesitated, but only for an instant. He wanted with all his heart to go, and José's firm clasp, helping him to his feet, as though he weighed no more than a feather, dispersed his shyness, sent a reassuring thrill through him. They went to the potting shed, where José shouldered an open box of petunia seedlings, which the Consul had ordered him to bring that morning from the market, then proceeded to the far end of the lawn. Here, after stretching a double string along the freshly prepared plot, the gardener began to bed out the young plants. At first, Nicholas was content to watch, but presently, re-

23

sponding to José's glances of invitation, he bent down and timidly planted a seedling for himself. After that, he could not bring himself to stop. It was a lovely sensation to pick up the cool, green stem, to knead the soft, hot soil around the hairlike roots, to see the little shoot standing bravely up, resolved to face the world.

Nicholas had always lived in towns, in houses which gave directly on to the street, and now, squatting beside José, the sung beating warmly upon the back of his neck, the smell of the earth filling his nostrils with a kind of intoxication, he told himself that he had never known anything so wonderful. Even the pricking of perspiration beneath his undershirt, normally a portentous symptom, caused him no worry at all.

Towards four o'clock the planting was finished and, with real pride, Nicholas stood beside José, viewing the neatly spaced bed which would later on bloom into lovely, vivid colour. So immersed was the little boy that he did not hear the car as it entered the drive but, a minute later, he was startled by his father's voice behind him.

"Nicholas, what on earth are you doing?" The tone was surprised, tinged with disapproval.

He had jumped a little, though not much, and now he swung round with a face still lit by the joy of his achievement.

"Oh, Father, I've had such an interesting time. Watching, and helping too, with these petunias. And now they have to be watered, or they'll not thrive." He went on, coaxingly: "It isn't really late. May I just wait a moment and see them done?"

Displeased and uncertain, Brande gazed from his son to the Spanish gardener who, knowing his position, had withdrawn a few paces and was now winding the long string upon its wooden peg. Something impersonal and humble in that action seemed to reassure the Consul. His brow, which had borne a slight cloud, like a haze upon Olympus, gradually cleared. Raising his eyebrows, he answered dryly:

"Well, if you're not too long. And see you don't catch cold. Our heavy cases have arrived. I'm going in to unpack."

"Oh, thank you, Father," Nicholas exclaimed, clapping his hands. "I haven't in the least caught cold. I'll join you quite soon."

Harrington Brande turned and went indoors. Neatly arranged in the hall, three wooden boxes stood awaiting him with the lids and surplus straw already removed. Garcia, he reflected, was proving even more useful than he had hoped. He stepped to the bell-pull and summoned the man, then, alert for the safety of his greatest treasure, cast an exploratory eye upon the contents of the boxes. Ah, here it was—carefully, he withdrew from the smallest case a thick bundle of typescript bound with red tape.

"You rang, señor?"

Brande swung round.

"Ah, yes, Garcia. You've made an excellent beginning here. Now, will you take this? Gently, please. It is the manuscript of my book."

The butler widened his eyes.

"The señor is an author?"

Flattered by the exclamation, with its overtones of adulation, Harrington Brande inclined his head.

"For many years now I have been occupied with a considerable work . . . the biography of a great man."

"Does the señor mean himself?"

Brande laughed, actually laughed, with pleasure.

"Come, come, Garcia. You go a little too far. Find some strong wrapping paper and make a neat package. I want to take it to the office. Then come back and help me with my weapons."

"Of course, señor."

When the man had gone Brande stood for a minute, then moved to the nearest crate, probing amongst the contents, wondering where he should begin. But suddenly he paused, his eye caught by a cardboard folder which lay on top of the case. His face altered. A muttered exclamation broke from his lips. The packing had been done by a firm of Havre re-

25

movers and from the recesses of some drawer they had brought to light a photograph he long ago had banished from his sight. It was the likeness of his wife.

Slowly, as though it were a snake possessing the power to strike at him, he picked up the photograph and, with an expression that was strained and strangely haunted, steeled himself to look at it. Yes, there was Marion, with her pale, charming face and soft, dark eyes, her sensuous lips parted in that shadowy smile which had always baffled him. Still holding the photograph, he sat down broodingly in the window alcove, thinking of that first fateful evening when he had met her.

It was some ten years before at Bowdoin College, whither he had gone while on long leave from Washington to deliver a lecture to a student's society. At the reception which followed he had observed, standing near the door, this pale, rather thin girl, dressed in black—it appeared she was in mourning for her mother—and immediately a sensation had possessed him, an overflowing emotion which, in all his exact dealings with the other sex, he had never known before. He had had himself introduced, made guarded inquiries, discovered that she was poor, that her father, a superannuated university professor, lay ill of an incurable complaint in most indifferent lodgings in the town.

He then decided on a Maine vacation, found a good hotel in the vicinity and, in the most helpful manner imaginable, pressed his suit, not with much success, yet with a kind of precise tenacity. She told him she did not wish to marry. Twice she refused him, and though he went away, sore and rather sullen, for a month or two, still he came back, drawn by his passion and the steady ripening of her beauty. That winter, in February, her father died and she was alone. The opportunity was too favourable to miss. On the afternoon of the funeral, when she sat, solitary, silent, and wretched, watching the rain roll down the window panes, when her rented room, the slush and snow outside—when, indeed, all the circumstances of her life seemed more than usually

26

dreary, she had, with a strange passive look, yielded and accepted him.

And then, what had happened? God knew that he had done his utmost to prove his love—no one could have been more devoted. He was still stationed in Washington, his prospects were bright, their hotel apartment was agreeable. To the fullest extent of his means, he surrounded her with comfort, chose books and flowers for her, planned her entertainment, advised her on what people they should know, even helped her to select her dresses. He was with her everywhere, at all times—even at public functions, which he pressed her to attend, he was always at her side. And when they perforce were briefly separated, at dinner, or in the crowded reception rooms, he followed her with a deep, possessive yearning, careless of who should see how desirable, how necessary she had become to him.

She was more silent than he could have believed, and indeed these silences grew, but as he liked to talk that did not distress him. Occasionally, when at some length he had impressed upon her his point of view, in politics perhaps, or art, or, say, personal hygiene, the look in her eyes made him uncomfortable, and her shadowy smile was always baffling. But never, never could he have anticipated that evening, some months after the birth of their child, when, with colourless face and nervously averted gaze, she had asked for a separate room. It rankled still, with the bitterness of a long-inflicted injury.

"Why?" he had stammered with a livid face. "Aren't you my wife?"

She answered in a voice so low it was almost inaudible:

"Sometimes I should like to belong a little to myself."

Of course, he had not consented. She was his lawful helpmate and he had his rights. But he had sensed then, for the first time, her aversion to him, a strange and incredible antipathy, a barrier which grew, despite his efforts to break it down, to possess her completely, bodily and spiritually, as his own.

27

He was a virile man, capable surely of compelling desire, of fulfilling his part in the world of the senses. Yet how often, balanced upon the moment of final fulfilment, would he emerge suddenly from his own pleasure, shocked by the frightful knowledge that he was alone, that she lay with clenched teeth, rigid and motionless as a corpse, cast there by some icy sea.

Although in his heart he knew it to be absurd, he had been goaded to suspect that she must have a lover, had watched her jealously, had gone so far—was he not her husband?—as to set an agent to spy upon her movements. All to no purpose. Could it be, simply, that she detested him?

Then he had been transferred to Europe and the steady succession of his 'moves' had taken them to Stuttgart, Liége, Ancona . . . places which, he told her bitterly, any normal, loving woman would have found attractive in his company. Was she pining for her homeland? The thought helped him at times, salvaged in some degree his wounded pride. And when he was granted an extra leave he took her, and Nicholas, now aged three, back to America. Alas! it was there that he received the final blow. One day she had come into the rented New York apartment and, with faintly hollowed cheeks and drooping head, had said that, for the time being, she must leave him. The strain of their life together had broken her nerve—she must be alone, for some months, to readjust herself.

He had felt himself turn cold, sick with a longing to crush her brutally in his arms. Sweeping aside her pleading, he had delivered his ultimatum coldly:

"If you go, I'll not take you back. With me it's all or nothing."

She made no reply. But he could still see her shadowy eyes, holding the eternal enigma which had always tortured him. He went on, biting his lip until it bled:

"You'll have no money, no position. And no hand, none, in bringing up our child."

28

"Have I got that now?" she answered sadly and, turning, went slowly from the room.

Here, in the embrasure of this Spanish house, with his head buried in his hands, he could still see her slender, swaying figure, dressed in grey, could still breathe in the warmth and perfume of her presence. Well, she was gone, completely eradicted from his life. When last, indirectly, he had heard of her she was rooming in a woman's boarding-house in New York, working—for a pittance, he presumed—in a communal welfare centre. So be it, then. At least he had what she had not, their son. All that love which she had spurned was now transferred, lavished upon Nicholas. He adored the boy, he would not deny it, and he would cherish him, hold him close to his heart, always . . . always.

For long moments he remained there, bowed and brooding, the lines of his face drawn back in hungry longing, his lips twisted in something like a sneer. Suddenly there came the sound of laughter from without. Recalled, he raised his head, gazed heavily through the window, perceived José and his son, carrying the watering can along the garden path together, sharing a joke which apparently amused them both.

The Consul's cheek twitched as though, unexpectantly, he had suffered another wound. Abruptly he rose, went to the door and, controlling his voice, called out:

"Nicholas, come in, my dear. Come in at once."

FOUR

IT WAS TEN o'clock on Sunday morning, some three weeks later, and the Consul sat restfully at breakfast with his son in the sunlit alcove of the dining-room. Outside, the spring, exquisite as a bride, was unfolding a day so lovely that little Nicholas had longed to take his toast and honey on the open veranda. But his father, wary of the early deceitful air, had chidingly shaken his head. Instead, he had ordered Garcia to set a small table by the window. Here, at least, the boy could view the bright flashing of the scarlet tanagers amongst the mimosa shrubs and hear the tender, far-off pealing of the church bells.

"Father." From time to time Nicholas had been glancing at the Consul who, in his most favourable humour, was now agreeably occupied with a light Larranaga cigar and his two-day-old copy of the *Echo de Paris*—he judged only this journal worth his attention and had his friend Halevy send him a copy once a week. "Father, I should like so much to go to the *pelota* game this afternoon."

Slowly the Consul lowered his paper.

"The *pelota* game." He repeated without comprehension.

"Yes, Father." The blood had rushed into the small boy's cheeks, but he summoned his courage and went on: "It is a kind of handball which they play here. Very fast and exciting. All the towns on Costa Brava are in the league. And to-day Huesca, the champions, are meeting San Jorge."

Harrington Brande was gazing in amazement at his son's eager face. Gradually his expression relaxed.

"Well, well!" he exclaimed mildly. "So Garcia has been talking to you. What nonsense goes on here when I'm at the office! Tell me, where and when is this famous game to take place?"

"At the Recreo, Father," Nicholas breathed, not daring to confess that Garcia was not his informant. "Four o'clock this afternoon. Oh, do let us go."

The suspicion of a smile hovered about the Consul's mobile lips. It gratified him that his dear child should voluntarily seek out his companionship.

"Well." He appeared to consider. "If you take your tonic now . . . finish your Spanish composition . . . and rest for an hour after lunch, then we shall see."

"Oh, thank you, thank you, Father." Nicholas jumped up, delighted.

At half-past three that afternoon the two set off, Nicholas in the highest spirits, Mr. Brande exhibiting a mood of in-

30

dulgent good humour. The Consul knew nothing of sport. Once at Ancona he had thrown the first pitch at a baseball game arranged between teams drawn from visiting United States naval forces and again, some years later at Knocke, he had presented the prizes at the local sailing club's regatta. Now, however, in an amused fashion, he subscribed to something of his son's expectation.

They parked the car in the Plaza, and by traversing a network of narrow streets behind the fruit market came out at the Recreo, which, Mr. Brande noted with faint misgiving, stood in a low part of the town. It was, indeed, an indifferent enclosure, fenced by a wooden paling stuck over with bills advertising the local theatre and the forthcoming April *corridas* at Barcelona. Nevertheless, the Consul willingly enough permitted himself to be tugged by Nicholas to the front row of the *tribuna*, a backless wooden plank which faced directly on to the concrete court, where a man in shirtsleeves with a pot of red paint, was freshening up the lines.

They were early. Only a few youths had gathered on the top tier of benches where, with their feet up, they were smoking, chewing dried locust pods, joking loudly, and arguing in a regrettably vulgar manner. From time to time other spectators, with hands in their pockets, strolled in, mostly young men and boys who took their places at the rear and joined in the general rowdiness. The Consul reflected that at least they were some distance from these cads and had adequate space in which to avoid contact with them. But, alas! no sooner had four o'clock struck upon the Marina clock than the real *aficionados* broke in upon the *tribuna*, a crowding, chattering mass of humanity, pushing and elbowing into every available vacant space. In no time at all, the benches were packed, the aisles full of squatting human forms. A stout little man in a battered black sombrero and shiny dark suit, with half an onion in one hand and a hunk of bread in the other, squeezed himself into position beside the Consul and with a friendly grin sharpened his clasp-knife upon his boot and began noisily to eat. Small whistles broke out all over the arena,

31

accompanied by a slow rhythmic stamping of feet and cries of "*Olé . . . Olé . . . Olé. . . .*"

"They'll soon start now, Father. Shall I explain about the game?" Nicholas leaned forward and pointed eagerly across the court. "You see these two walls. They're set exactly opposite each other, about two hundred feet apart. One's called the *frontis* and the other the *pareo de rebote*. These red lines on them show the space where the ball must strike. And the red lines on the court itself—they call it the *concha*—mark out the same thing. If the ball bounces outside them it's a fault and counts a point to the other side."

While the Consul stared in stiff curiosity, the boy rattled on.

"There are two players on each side, the *delantaro*—that's the forward—and the *zaquero*, the back. Huesca play in blue shirts, San Jorge in white. The *pelota*—that's the ball—is made of india-rubber, bound with yarn and covered with sheepskin, and they throw it with the *cesta*. The play is fast, oh, terribly fast. . . ."

At this point, in sudden interruption, there came a concerted shout from the crowd and, vaulting over the barrier on the opposite side of the concrete rectangle, the four players appeared upon the court. They wore singlets and white linen trousers, and fastened to the right hand of each, by means of a glove attachment, was a kind of light wickerwork basket. As they began a swift practice knock-up against the walls, the Consul felt Nicholas grow tense beside him.

"Now you see, Father. You see why we came. Isn't it a surprise for you? Isn't it splendid?"

At first Brande did not understand but, following the child's glowing gaze, he saw that it was fixed magnetically upon the younger of the two San Jorge players, a tall, lithe figure, moving with graceful ease about the court. It was José.

The Consul started, lost countenance, and for a long moment remained quite motionless. In a flash of understanding the situation became clear to him—the boy's eagerness to

32

come to the match, his extraordinary knowledge of the game, his undreamed-of, yet unmistakable, complicity with the young gardener.

"Look, look, Father," Nicholas shrilled. "They're starting now. And José's seen us. He just waved his hand to me."

Out on the court the forward of the Huesca side had taken his position at the mark and amidst a sudden stillness he bounced the *pelota* once, then shot it hard against the wall. Dully, Harrington Brande followed the flight of the ball, as with incredible speed it flew back and forth. He was conscious of a hurt, tight feeling in his chest, which hindered his breathing, and increased his existing sense of oppression. Had they not been wedged irremovably by the mob he would have risen and led his son from this odious enclosure. Instead, although aware that he would thus intensify his hurt, the Consul glanced sideways at the boy who, poised upon the edge of the bench, quite unmindful of any discomfort, was thrillingly absorbed in the progress of the contest. With bright eye and parted lips, his small fists clenching and unclenching, he swayed and stiffened in unison with the others, muttering intent exclamations of approval or dismay, and even, from time to time, joining his high treble shamelessly to the swelling vociferations of the crowd.

"*Olé. Olé*. Come on, San Jorge. Played . . . oh, well played, José *amigo*."

With an effort, Harrington Brande withdrew his gaze and returned it to the court. Warmed to the game, the players were now fiercely engaged in a series of long rallies, flashing the *pelota* against the wall from every angle of *concha*. It was incredible, the skill with which they caught the ball, not holding it even for an instant in the basket, before they sped it back, fast and true, like a bullet, to the mark. The sides, Brande could see, were evenly matched indeed, and the figures on the score board at this moment showed a tally of 19 all.

Both the Huesca men were young and agile. The San Jorge back, on the other hand, was middle-aged, a short and

33

swarthy fellow with a cropped head and bandy legs, who played with great astuteness and experience, yet whose lack of speed prevented him from covering his proper section of the court. It fell, therefore, to his partner to offset this handicap and, as the Consul watched, in gloomy averseness, José's flowing action, the instinctive sureness of his touch, he could not but acknowledge that the youth surpassed by far the other players on the court. And with this came a sudden desire that San Jorge should be defeated in the match.

With an expressionless face—his chill official manner—Harrington Brande began to follow closely every stroke, every point of the game. The score was now 35 to 32 in favour of the Huesca pair who, with commendable strategy, were concentrating volley after volley upon the San Jorge back. Under this relentless attack and the weight of his years, the older player was perceptibly tiring and Brande smiled grimly within himself as the local supporters began to shout, swear and shower execrations upon his grizzled head.

"*Olé ... Olé. ...* Use thyself, Jaime. Run, old son of a dog. Come, José *amigo*; for the love of God save us from disgrace."

Under these exhortations it seemed that José was everywhere on the court, gliding, stretching, striking, always with that faint, gentle smile, even though his breath came quickly and the perspiration ran from every pore. But despite his efforts the Huesca men clung desperately to their lead and the score rose steadily, ominously, until it stood at 48 to 46.

The crowd was now in constant uproar, yelling, gesticulating, beseeching and reviling with Latin intensity. And little Nicholas, pale with excitement, was shouting his heart out with the rest.

"Come on, San Jorge. Come on, José. We want you to win ... to win ... to win."

At this, the Huesca forward played a deceptive drop shot and Jaime, completely winded, failed with the return. He threw up his hands to indicate despair and a groan broke

34

from the San Jorge supporters. One more point would give Huesca the match.

Forwards and backwards went the *pelota* in what might well be the final rally. Suddenly the Huesca leader, leaping, slipped on the concrete, and missed the ball. He rose at once, unhurt, with a confident wave to his followers. But no sooner had he restarted the play than José aced him with a cannon-ball return. An anxious cheer went up from the crowd. The score was now 49 to 48.

In a queer silence, José went to the mark to serve. A profound stillness lay over the packed arena as the rally began. It was unendurably protracted, in a mounting anguish of excitement and suspense. The Huesca men were playing safely, depending upon their opponents to make a fault, while José, upon whom the burden of responsibility had fallen, seemed equally resolved to take no risks. Steadily, steadily went the exchanges, till suddenly, breaking that measured rhythm, José's long arm unexpectedly lashed out and with a change of pace he angled the ball between his two opponents. The score was level at 49 all.

Now no one dared to take a breath. They were all standing up, craning forward, watching the flying ball as it ricocheted between the walls. Huesca, with the courage of desperation, had thrown caution to the winds in a brilliant volleying action. Once, twice, they made shots which seemed certain aces, but José, as though inspired, succeeded somehow in making a safe return. Finally there came a wide, swifty volley that looked well beyond his reach. He leaped high, high into the air, swung with all his strength, and crashed the ball home for the winning point.

A long, low sigh ascended to the sky. Then pandemonium broke loose. Men threw their hats into the air, wept, laughed, embraced each other, and shouted in a kind of delirious ecstasy.

Nicholas, standing up bright-eyed on the bench, kept swinging his arms, and crying wildly:

35

"Hurrah! Hurrah! I knew he'd do it! I knew! I knew! Hurrah!"

As the players, limp and exhausted, walked off the court the crowd scaled the barrier and swarmed upon them. In an instant José was surrounded, hugged, kissed and pounded, then, as he cried out for mercy, hoisted shoulder high and borne from the enclosure.

"Oh, Father," Nicholas gasped, getting down at last. "Wasn't that wonderful? I'm so glad you took me."

The Consul answered with a rigid smile. The climax of the game and the succeeding demonstration had caused him the deepest mortification. Yet not for the world would he have revealed the strange, inexplicable bitterness which rankled within his breast. He took his son's hand and, as the crowd had now thinned, proceeded in silence towards the Plaza.

"Really, it was a victory for us," Nicholas chattered as they got into the car. "For José belongs to our establishment. And it was he who won the game."

Without answer, Harrington Brande stabbed the self-starter. And as he drove off, gazing straight ahead, the little boy began, doubtfully, to steal glances at him, wondering if he had, inadvertently, given offence.

"Is anything wrong, Father?" he asked, at last.

There was a perceptible pause.

"No, Nicholas, nothing is wrong, except that I have a splitting headache. You see, I am not used to being crushed in with the common herd, or to being pushed, elbowed and kicked for the sake of a stupid game."

"But, Father . . ." Nicholas, confounded, was about to make some protest, but the sight of that chilly profile caused him to break off.

Dinner was ready when they reached home. But the silence continued through the meal—one of those aloof and frozen silences which the Consul periodically imposed, when he seemed to retreat far within himself and to gaze through persons and objects as though viewing, like an outraged god, only those things which were empyrean and eternal.

"Shall I go upstairs now, Father?" Nicholas asked, in a subdued voice, when he had drained the last of his milk.

"As you please."

Slowly and sadly, the little boy mounted the wide, dark walnut stairway. The joy of the day, with its excitement and novelty, its overtones and lustre, was quenched within him. He forgot about José and the game, could think only of his father's stern, afflicted face. Accustomed to the joint ritual of the evening, he felt himself disowned and deserted in the great shadowy bedroom. He undressed listlessly, washed, and pulled on his nightshirt. Then, turning, he saw the Consul in the doorway.

"Oh, Father." He gulped with relief. "I thought you wouldn't come."

The Consul answered gravely:

"*I* am not likely to fail in my duty, Nicholas."

"I'm sorry if I've done anything, really I am, Father." It was hard for him to keep back his tears. "But I . . . I don't know what it is."

"Kneel for your prayers." The Consul took his usual place, laid an arm upon the boy's shoulders, his tone turning low. "You are growing up now, Nicholas. You must be aware how painful and difficult are the circumstances of my life. You know the burden I have borne since . . . since your mother left us. Lately my insomnia, increased by my literary labours, has become a perfect martyrdom. There are days when I am so overcome by suffering and exhaustion I can barely concentrate upon my work. And yet . . ." The Consul lifted a knitted brow. "In spite of all this, I have devoted, consecrated myself unswervingly, to you."

The little boy hung his head. Tears, like crystal dewdrops, were forming upon his soft lashes.

"Yes, Nicholas, I have been not only your father, but your friend, your teacher, your nurse. I do not deny that I have drawn from this dedicated service a deep felicity . . . a gladness and refreshment which brought balm to my wounded soul. It is, my dear child, a labour of love. Yet even the most un-

37

selfish passion demands some slight affection in return. That is why, to-day, my heart has been rent by the thought that ... you do not care for me."

"No, no, Father," Nicholas cried out, finding words at last. "It's not true. How can you believe such a thing?"

A strange flicker passed across the crucified face.

"Some things are intangible, my child. A careless word ... a look ... a chance gesture. ..."

"No, no," Nicholas almost shouted. "I do love you, you know I do. Mother treated you abominably. But I won't. We'll always be together." Weeping hysterically, his body shaking, Nicholas reached up and threw his arms round his father's neck.

"My own boy," the Consul murmured, holding closely against him that slight, living burden. As he felt, upon his breast, the birdlike flutter of the childish heart, an invading warmth melted the pain within him. He sighed deeply and closed his eyes.

At last he gently disengaged himself, spoke with a tender smile.

"Now say your prayers, dear child, and I will read to you."

FIVE

YET THROUGH THE sweetness of this reconciliation, the fond knowledge that Nicholas was more completely attached to him than ever, the Consul could not forget the part played by José in that painful, if brief, estrangement. It had been his practice as he left the villa in the morning to acknowledge, distantly, his gardener's respectful salute. Now, however, he passed by with studied indifference, his face averted, eyes fixed straight ahead, as though to avoid seeing him. Yet in that brief moment, he was acutely conscious of the youth, of his young figure under the light cotton, the vigorous sweep of his arms as he swung the long scythe, his warmly ingenuous smile. And a surge of resentment went through his

38

veins, an irritation that remained with him long after he had reached the office.

He tried to shake off his emotion. It was preposterous that he should permit himself to be disturbed by a mere servant, a common youngster from the town, and quite beneath his dignity to take any action in a matter which, after all, seemed less important when viewed in retrospect. Doubtless the fellow had bragged to Nicholas about his prowess at *pelota* and had urged him to come to watch him play the game. No more than that. Nevertheless, despite this reasoning, there remained in the Consul's breast that strange sense of jealousy, and an animosity, which, as though it fed upon itself, seemed to grow from day to day.

For a while José noticed nothing, but as one morning succeeded another and still his master passed him with that blank, impervious frown, he began to fear that he was failing to give satisfaction, and his simple heart was filled with apprehension. Work was scarce in San Jorge, good situations difficult to find, and he had his mother, Maria, to think of, to say nothing of his sisters, and old Pedro, his grandfather, who had not done a stroke for seven years. Alarmed, he increased his already strenuous efforts, arrived half an hour earlier than the stipulated time, departed only when dusk began to fall.

One morning, as he worked into an uncleared patch beyond the rocky wall, he saw deep in the mossy shelter of some myrtle shrubs three fragile white stars, still damp with dew, the first freesias. His eyes lit up with pleasure, he stood in admiration for a long moment, then nodded to himself, crushed into the undergrowth, and carefully picked the flowers. In the toolshed, whistling under his breath, he bound them neatly with raffia against a light spray of fern. Smartening his hair before the broken scrap of mirror, he hastened to the front porch. He had not long to wait before his master appeared on the veranda.

"*Señor*," José said, and stopped, finding it too difficult to make the agreeable speech which he had prepared. He simply

39

smiled, with touching diffidence, and handed up the *boutonnière*.

There was a pause. The Consul, like one forced against his will, slowly turned, and for the first time, since the *pelota* game, looked directly at the youth. This action, which seemed to break down some deep-seated and primitive inhibition, produced in him a curious sense of liberation, of mastery. His sense of tension, so long suppressed, was suddenly dissolved and, instead, he felt himself capable of an almost superhuman calm.

"What is this?" he inquired formally.

"For your pleasure, *señor* . . . to wear. The first freesias of spring."

"You picked them . . . these flowers?"

"But . . . yes, *señor*."

"You have no right to do such a thing. These flowers are mine. I do not wish them picked. I wish them to remain growing in the garden, where they properly belong."

"But, *señor* . . ." José faltered.

"That is enough. You are a stupid, self-willed fellow. You exceed your position. Let us have no more of it in future. Do you understand?"

Under the Consul's cold, steady gaze, José's hurt eyes fell, his lithe young figure appeared to droop, to lose virility and poise. Sadly cast down, he looked at the little bunch of perfumed blossoms, whose stems had grown warm in his perspiring hands, and, as though not knowing what to do with this rejected offering, he placed it confusedly behind his ear. As he moved off, clumsily, to the myrtle patch, he perceived that Garcia, waiting beside the car, with that peculiar grimace, sardonic and at the same time blank, which gave to the impassive face a look of cruelty, had witnessed his humiliation. He bit his lip and turned away his head, as though to hide his burning cheeks.

The Consul drove to the town, sitting erect in the rear seat of his open automobile with the folding windscreen lowered, the breeze blowing pleasantly about him. He felt eased and

40

satisfied, like a man who has thrown off an irritating garment and now finds himself restored to comfort and normality. So agreeable was his humour that, when he entered the office and found Alvin Burton already bent over a pile of bills of lading in the outer room, he paused and, with a touch of compunction, remarked:

"Good morning, Burton. By the way, it's about time you and your wife came to see us at Casa Breza." As his assistant started up in pleased surprise, he continued generously: "Come next Sunday, won't you? Come in the afternoon and we'll give you tea."

"Oh, thank you, sir," Alvin exclaimed, deeply gratified. "Thank you ever so much. I know that Mrs. Burton . . ."

"Quite," the Consul cut in blandly. "We shall expect you both at five o'clock. Don't be late."

He passed into his private office, where a fresh copy of the *Echo de Paris*, the wrapper carefully removed, lay upon his desk. But his present mood was too creative to waste upon the news-sheet. A quick survey showed that there was nothing of importance in his official mail. He sat down in his swivel chair and, permitting himself one of his rare departures from his punctilious routine, he drew out from the bottom drawer the package he had brought from the villa the day before—his manuscript on Malbranche.

To the rest of the world Nicholas Malbranche might be a dim, an unknown figure, but to Harrington Brande this forgotten Frenchman, who in the eighteenth century attempted to adopt the teachings of Descartes in the interests of theology, had become an exemplar, in whose pedantic philosophy he found a pattern for his behaviour, the sonorous echo of his own soul. That Malbranche should be so utterly neglected served merely to fan his ardour, to increase his pride that he, personally, would be hailed as the discoverer who had brought this paragon from obscurity into the bright light of day.

Over the past ten years, with mounting ambition, he had laboured prodigiously upon the compilation of a life of his

41

hero. Several times he had sent the first half of his manuscript to leading publishing houses. The lack of response—none had evinced the slightest interest—was bitterly provoking, for he was not impervious to the flight of time or the success of others, yet it had neither surprised nor deterred the Consul. He considered the work too erudite to be vulgarly popular and, if necessary, proposed to produce it at his own expense, confident that when it reached the hands of the inner circle of European savants it would be instantly acclaimed. As a gesture of proud defiance he had named his son Francis Nicholas, despite the protests of his wife, whose lack of enthusiasm for his project had been, alas! but one of her lamentable disloyalties. Never, indeed, would he forgive her that episode when having, in the first flush of his love, permitted her to read some chapters of the masterpiece, he had pressed confidently for her opinion.

"I'm afraid I don't know enough about it," she had answered evasively.

"Naturally, I don't expect you to understand the philosophy, my dear. But the style . . . the drama . . . the movement . . . of the book?"

"No, really, Harrington . . . I'm no judge. . . ."

"Oh, come now." He laughed playfully, fondling her hand. "Be as critical as you like. Speak the truth."

A difficult silence had followed. Then, cornered, she had smiled her shadowy smile, as though begging his forgiveness.

"If you really insist, Harrington, I'm afraid it bored me frightfully."

Ah, well, Malbranche had also had his Calvary. And now, all that was past, the manuscript was near completion and, as though in anticipation of his triumphant vindication, the Consul firmly took up his pen. But as he did so, unexpectedly he paused, and raised his head. As though seeing again that bar of humiliation upon José's brow, his eyes turned distant, strangely light, in his sallow face. Then, slowly, as he began to write, he smiled.

42

SIX

WHEN SUNDAY CAME the Consul decided that he would receive the Burtons out of doors and give them tea in the garden. The afternoon was fine and warm; moreover, since twilight still fell early, his guests would thus have less opportunity to settle down and overstay their welcome. He ordered Garcia to arrange a table in the arbour, and to set out sandwiches, buttered rolls, and some of those local iced cakes called *pan de jabon*, which he fancied might suit Mrs. Burton's taste.

As the hour drew near he was in an excellent humour. He had spent a delightful day with Nicholas, just the two of them together, perusing a folio of eighteenth-century Andalusian prints which, like a true connoisseur, he had picked up for a few pesos from a little shop near the Consulate. Now, gazing across the arbour at his son, who looked particularly neat in a navy blue suit and stiff white collar, he was struck by the improvement in the boy's health. That air of delicate fragility had lessened, and the sickly pallor of his skin was now replaced by a tinge of healthy brown. Why, even his narrow shoulders seemed somehow to have acquired a more decided set. One must not run too fast, of course. Yet it was a profound satisfaction that Nicholas should at last be responding to the care he had so constantly bestowed upon him.

Alvin and his wife arrived, punctually, in a hired car and, having received them graciously, the Consul proposed a stroll round the garden. While Alvin and Nicholas went ahead, he followed, more slowly, with Mrs. Burton. She was a quiet young woman with glasses and a fresh complexion, pretty enough, he supposed, in an ordinary sort of way, wearing a modest brown voile dress which he shrewdly guessed she had cut from paper patterns and made at home. Apparently she came from a small town in Michigan, was one of a large

43

family, and had met Alvin on the campus of the State University. That she seemed sensible and good-natured did not prevent him from immediately classifying her as nondescript. Still, her anxiety to please was gratifying. Because of this, he set out to make himself agreeable and when they sat down to tea in the arbour he turned to her in his best style:

"Perhaps you would be kind enough to be our hostess? As you know, our establishment here is only a bachelor one. We miss the refinements of feminine society."

It amused him mildly to observe how she responded to this attention, filling and passing the teacups with awkward shyness. And again, in the desire to demonstrate his own powers, he began to talk in his most captivating manner. He was, when he chose, an interesting conversationalist, and now he exerted himself, drawing freely upon the lighter side of his experience, exhibiting himself in the role of learned gentleman and benevolent counsellor, relating little anecdotes, painting a picture of his life in Europe which was perhaps more glamorous than accurate.

"Oh, how wonderful!" Alvin sighed as the Consul concluded an account of the coronation of King Albert which he had witnessed in the Cathedral at Brussels during his sojourn in Belgium. "We'd have given anything to be present at such a colourful ceremony. Wouldn't we, Carol?"

"Yes," she agreed warmly, with downcast eyes.

"Your chance will come," Brande suggested helpfully.

"Oh, we hope so! Don't we, honey?"

She did not answer, but directed towards her husband a glance of such intimate tenderness that the Consul, who could never see a happy marriage without thinking of the failure of his own, felt a sudden stab of pain. They had only been married eighteen months, of course, yet they were obviously deeply attached to one another. Why was it that this nervous nonentity, who stammered when anyone spoke sharply to him and was often ridiculously adolescent in his behaviour, could command such wifely affection while he,

44

superior in every way, had failed so utterly to hold the one woman he had ever loved?

With a cynicism he scarcely would have suspected in himself, he turned to Mrs. Burton.

"It hadn't struck me before," he said, in his blandest voice, "but San Jorge must be rather a dull place for a woman."

A swift surprise showed in her grey, short-sighted eyes.

"Oh no . . . not at all, sir."

That she should call him 'sir' made him feel old, caused him another pang.

"She has the apartment to look after," Burton said fondly. "And I must say she's made it real homey."

"Homey," the Consul echoed in an indescribable tone.

"Yes, sir. As I told you, it's small, but it's very snug."

"Still, I should imagine a young couple wouldn't find much social life here," persisted the Consul, "cramped in the back street of a dingy little Spanish town."

For the first time Carol Burton looked at him directly. Was it possible, he asked himself, that despite the amiable blankness of his expression she surmised the deeper intention of his remark? She answered quickly:

"We have lots of friends, sir, I assure you. They aren't very grand, but they're nice . . . the baker and the grocer, the old priest, Father Limaza, the cigarette-maker downstairs. We go sailing often in the bay with Miguel, the Alcade's son. In the evenings we sometimes drop in at the Teatro—these old Spanish movies are tremendous fun—and afterwards we have supper at the Chantaco. You ought to taste the iced beer there; it's first-rate. Then we've started a little club for the local boys and girls. We have ping-pong and ninepins. I give them ice-cream and Alvin even tries to teach them baseball." Her colour had risen. She went on earnestly, a little unguardedly; "We'd be so glad to see Nicholas there. He'd enjoy the other children . . . especially if he feels lonely out here."

After that there was a pause. The Consul's expression had

45

turned stiff. Send Nicholas amongst these common brats, indeed! Only the sacred obligations of hospitality held back a sharp expression of his indignation. Yet everything, thought Alvin ingenuously, had passed off extremely well. For a little while he devoted himself, with Carol, to Nicholas, then, with a deferential air, he glanced at his watch.

"We must not keep you too long, sir. It's really time we were going."

They were about to rise when steps sounded on the cobbled yard and Nicholas, who had for some time been searching the garden with expectant glances, suddenly lost that air of preoccupation which he had worn for most of the afternoon.

"Look!" he exclaimed, eagerly. "There he is! I believe he's got some after all." And before his father could prevent him, he beckoned excitedly and called out in a shrill voice: "José! José! Come over here."

There was an amazed silence. The Consul drew himself up with a heavy frown.

"What do you mean, Nicholas? Be quiet at once," he commanded harshly. But he was too late.

From the shelter of the stableyard where he was hovering, in a state of indecision, José started forward, modestly, yet with a smile of triumph, towards the group. He wore his Sunday clothes, his Catalan hat flat upon his ears, and he carried in his hand a bundle wrapped in green osiers.

Unbelievingly, his eyes fixed, lips tightly compressed, Brande stared at the advancing youth who had materialised, so unexpectedly, at the summons of his son. Why was he here, on Sunday, at this hour? A strange chill fell upon him. And as if that were not enough, there was Nicholas, jumping in his seat and shouting rudely before their guests:

"Hurrah! Well done, José."

"Will you be quiet?" Brande said again in a low, intense tone.

José had now reached the arbour and with a little bow, like some rustic *matador*, he removed his absurd hat and thrust it beneath his left arm. He had smiled first to Nicholas, but

46

now his eyes, intent and serious, were bent propitiatingly upon the Consul.

"*Señor*," he began, "please to pardon me for disturbing you. I bring you a small gift. The flowers were not mine, and I did wrong to pick them, for which I am sorry. But these are mine, *señor*, and I beg you to accept them."

Opening the bundle of osiers, he displayed, not without pride, two fine trout, plump and pinkly speckled, lying side by side on some sprigs of wild mint.

Rigid and motionless, the Consul made no response, but Nicholas, leaning forward in ardent interest, broke out with increased animation.

"What beauties, José. And such big ones. Did you get them in the mill-pool or in the fast water above? Tell me, quick."

As though conscious, for the first time, of all their eyes upon him, José coloured slightly and moved his heavy boots, which were bronzed with yellow dust, creased by darker lines of sweat.

"In the fast water," he answered, smiling again at Nicholas, then went on, as though explaining, to the others. "It is a stream I go to, the Arengo, far back in the mountains. High up and crystal clear—oh, most beautiful, I assure you. But the trout are difficult. All morning I thought I should catch nothing. Then just before leaving I got these, each one more than a kilo." His warm gaze came to rest upon the Consul, he wiped the perspiration from his upper lip. "They are completely fresh, *señor*. I trust you will enjoy them."

Harrington Brande sat with his hands resting on the table, perfectly still, like a statue, perhaps the statue of a great man, upon a pediment in the public square. His face wore a marbled hardness too, but beneath, his pulse was pounding in his temples and all his blood seemed turned into gall.

"I am sorry," he said, at last, in a forced voice. "I never eat trout. And they are too rich for my son."

"But these are white trout, *señor* . . . the real mountain *trucha* . . ." José faltered. "Very fine and delicate . . ."

"Thank you, no," said the Consul, and directed his gaze

47

with icy courtesy towards his guests. "It might be that you would care to have them?"

"Oh, not at all," Alvin Burton responded, hurriedly, in an uncomfortable voice.

"Then take them to the kitchen." The Consul returned his frozen eyes to José's dusky face. In spite of himself, he could not keep a sneer from his lips nor a faint tremor from his voice. "The servants may be able to use them."

"Oh, no, Father," Nicholas cried, in deep dismay. "José wants us to have them."

"You are on a diet. You cannot have them."

Tears started at the back of the little boy's eyes.

"But, Father . . ."

"Enough." The Consul's tone bit like acid. "You may leave us now, my man."

There was a short pause. José drew himself up as though fighting a sudden fatigue. His breast heaved painfully as he made the effort to speak, yet his words, though they came haltingly, had a strange and simple dignity:

"I am sorry to have displeased you, señor. I rose this morning while it was still dark and walked twelve kilometres to catch these fish for you." His orange complexion had taken on a mottled pallor and in his dark eyes there burned a sultry spark. "I should have known that they were not fine enough for you. Perhaps, therefore, you will permit me to take them home. We are very poor, señor, with many mouths to feed, and these fish would make a good meal for us."

He closed the green bundle and with a stiff little bow turned away. Nicholas, with a hot pain in his side, clenched his fists tightly.

"Never mind, José," he called out, loud and uncaring. "Eat them for your supper. And see that old Pedro has a bit."

Then, as José's figure disappeared, he rose to his feet, begged in a half-articulated voice to be excused, and dashed off to his room.

Only the Consul's pride helped him to command the situation. Despite the welter of emotion in his breast he

48

turned calmly, with a humorous shrug, to his guests.

"Children, nowadays, are unpredictable." He smiled amusedly. "With Nicholas, the more stupid a servant, the more he offers him his sympathy."

Continuing, with well-chosen phrases, he soon had them laughing at a story of another blundering servant he had once endured, an excitable Neapolitan who had been a ship's cook and whose foible it had been to keep a parrot in the pantry. His manner, as he rose to see them to the car, showed nothing of the chaos of sensations which whirled and writhed within him.

When they had driven off he stood, with compressed brows, staring unseeingly at the blue mountains, watered by the crystal Arengo, soaring to the vault of heaven, wrapped in their eternal haze.

SEVEN

NEXT MORNING BRANDE came down early to breakfast. He had feared that he might have a bad night, but, strangely, had slept heavily. Garcia brought coffee and fruit appetisingly arranged in a round silver dish, then stood to serve him, silent and impassive, in the background. And now, considering the man's reserve, his dark and distant manner, reflecting indeed upon the whole pattern of his service with 'superior' families, wherein no doubt many secrets had come his way, only to be sealed behind these impenetrable lips, the Consul decided to confide in him.

"Garcia," he said, "I wish to ask you something."

The butler stepped forward without speaking, impersonal and inscrutable.

"It concerns José, the new gardener." Brande made pretence of stirring his coffee. "Have you seen him conversing, at any time, with my son?"

There was a pause. No shadow of a smile appeared on

Garcia's unruffled features, not a muscle of his pale face moved.

"At any time, Señor Brande? At all times would be the proper answer. They are continually together . . . talking, laughing, even working together."

"Working!" Despite Brande's effort to be casual, he choked a little on the word.

"Why, yes. And hard work too." The butler spoke in a toneless voice but all the time he watched the Consul intently, his eyes narrowed, like a cat. "Last week the little boy had his shirt off. I saw him from my window, bare to the waist, swinging a machete in the hot sun."

"Why did you not tell me?" asked the Consul, with knitted forehead.

"I am no tale-bearer." Garcia shrugged indifferently. "All the same, I do not like it. I know your son is delicate . . . sensitive . . . impressionable. And this José . . . I ask you, señor, what is he?"

A silence fell while the Consul restlessly revolved his spoon between his fingers. He dared not question the butler further.

"Thank you, Garcia," he said at last. "You have helped me considerably. I rely upon your discretion."

In reply, the man bowed with his usual deference, but as he turned away a gleam shone in his slanting eyes and that silent laugh creased his smooth face, making it a mask of mockery.

Left alone, Harrington Brande had no stomach for his customary after-breakfast cigar but sat drumming the table with taut fingers. His first impulse was to dismiss José at once, to be rid of him for ever. Yet, on reflection, he saw that such a simple step would not resolve his difficulty. Madness though it might seem, a struggle had developed between this low fellow and himself, latent perhaps, yet none the less real, for the affection and regard of Nicholas. Should he prejudice his position, stigmatise himself as an unjust master, and make a martyr of the youth by sending him away without proper pretext? A thousand times, no. Sooner or later this

50

situation might arise again. He would have to fight, somewhere, to retain his son's love, and perhaps against a more formidable opponent. Therefore he preferred to face the issue now, under conditions which suited him. As he reached this decision his heart beat faster and heavier with the swelling, secret desire to punish his enemy, to beat him down and break his spirit.

When he went off in the car, out of the corner of his eye he perceived the gardener watering the petunia beds, but he gave no sign of having seen him. That afternoon, however, after much restless meditation in the office, he returned a full hour before his usual time, hoping to surprise José and his son together. But Nicholas was upstairs, at his lessons, and the gardener stood alone, in the long grass beside the wall, sharpening his short scythe with absent, almost indolent strokes. Harrington Brande strode directly towards him.

"I wish to talk to you."

"Yes, señor." The tone was quietly respectful, the hot glint which had flashed in those dark pupils the day before was gone, yet there could be sensed a new firmness in the youth's expression, an independence, a kind of wary doggedness which whetted the edge of the Consul's anger. He said, deliberately:

"I forbid you to speak to Nicholas."

José studied his honing stone for a moment.

"God gave me a tongue, señor. Do you prohibit me from using it?"

"Yes," said the Consul, violently. "So far as my son is concerned. And on no account must you set him to work. You have been making him dig and hoe and hack down bushes."

"I have only been trying to make him strong," José answered. "So that he should not be all the time on his back like a sick girl."

"How dare you!"

"And he is better, much better already," José stubbornly persisted. "You can see for yourself . . . how brown and well

51

he looks. And he loves to cut the bracken with the light sickle I made him . . . and to be about with me, using his muscles, in the good fresh air."

A burst of fury turned Brande livid, but by a tremendous effort he suppressed it. He said rigidly:

"Either you give me your promise or you leave my service immediately."

There was a long pause. José glanced at the Consul, glanced away, then, with a blank and expressionless face, he muttered:

"I promise."

A surge of power went through the Consul, intensifying his desire to wound, to press home his advantage and teach this young upstart a lesson he would not readily forget. As José prepared, somewhat sullenly, to resume his scything, he exclaimed, so abruptly that the youth winced:

"Wait! There is another matter. The garden is not looking so well as I expected. I am disappointed. Here, for instance." He pointed to an area of rough ground, not yet reclaimed, beyond the catalpa tree. "It is extremely bare. I have decided to make a rockery."

"A rockery, señor?" José echoed queerly.

"Yes. If you move those stones from the field, beyond the bluff there, you'd have all the material you need."

José turned his eyes in the direction indicated by the Consul.

"These stones are extremely heavy, señor."

"Are you afraid of hard work?" Brande sneered.

"I hope I have proved to you that I am not, señor." José spoke in a controlled voice, as though explaining something patiently to a child. "But for such an operation one would require several men, iron chains, and a crane."

"Nonsense! One good man could do it."

"You are a good man, señor," José returned, in that same mild tone. "Could you move these rocks?"

"Don't be insolent."

José caught his full lip between his white teeth and gazed

52

across the bluff towards the rocks strewn upon its heathy surface. They were large, sharp and rough, veined with jagged quartz; some were actually boulders, deeply bedded in that sinewy and flinty soil which, to make matters worse, contained the spreading roots of some old, cut-down eucalyptus trees. To upheave and move such monsters would spoil even the springiest muscles for the finer things in life, especially for *pelota*. Merely to consider it made the youth feel beaten and sad. And yet, when he thought of his position at home, of his mother, on her knees all day at the public wash-station, of his five little sisters, whose mouths were always open, like young sparrows, to say nothing of old Pedro, who would never earn another penny in his life, he knew he must, at all costs, keep his position. Besides, there was Nicholas, whom he liked so much. . . . He raised his head . . . gravely . . . with a slow nobility.

"Very well, *señor*. I will do it."

"I thought you would," said Brande with a bitter, jeering smile. "See you make a good job of it. Or I'll know the reason why."

He turned and walked away, nodding agreeably to Garcia, who stood at the door waiting to take his hat and stick as he went in. To-night, after prayers, he would talk with Nicholas.

On the following morning José began to make the rockery. He had only the most rudimentary tools—a mattock, two light crowbars, and a wheelbarrow with a damaged axle. In most instances it was necessary to dig round the embedded boulder, to lever it up with the two iron bars, to lift or drag it on to the tilted wheelbarrow and then to trundle this unwieldy and precarious burden over fifty yards of rough ground to the selected site. Often, when a rock had been prised painfully from its bed it slipped at the last moment from the crowbars and sank more deeply into the earth. Or in transit it would topple, drunkenly, from the creaky wheelbarrow on to the hard drive so that it must be lifted back, strainingly, without any leverage to ease its insensate weight.

It was grilling work. The warm season was now at hand

53

and although the brief dawn came cool enough, soon the sun blazed out of a brilliant sky and waves of heat shimmered up like a mirage in the little garden. Blisters rose on José's hands, blood ran from a torn fingernail and dried in a brackish smear, perspiration broke out all over his young body. To keep the dripping moisture from his eyes, he tore his red cotton handkerchief and bound a strip about his forehead. Oh, the relief, the exquisite assuagement of that blessed moment when the orange sun finally dipped down behind the brimming sea.

Still, he would not, simply would not, give up; it was as though the bitter knowledge of injustice had steeled the gentle fibre of his spirit, and, as the days went by, he kept on, toiling at the killing task with a dogged and unflagging pride. Reclining in the arbour with his lesson books, pledged to unnatural silence, Nicholas watched his friend with straining eyes and throbbing, aching breast. He saw the weariness that slowed his steps. Once when a stone fell on José's foot his heart leaped agonisingly to his throat. And, worst of all, José did not look at him, did not even smile, but went to and fro, staring straight ahead with that same fixed expression on his suffering face.

A slow swell of feeling choked the little boy's heart. Though he could not, dared not, question the Consul's strict command, its purpose lay beyond his comprehension. He loved his father—of that there could not be the slightest doubt. Yet, in a different way, he cared for José too. Then why, oh why, was this chilling ban of silence imposed upon them? Suddenly, when he felt he could endure it no longer, an idea came to Nicholas, an inspiration, swift and splendid as a flash of light. It amazed him that he had not thought of it before. He need not disobey his father, yet he could break this horrible enforced estrangement with José after all. He lay for a moment, almost overcome, then quickly, reaching with trembling fingers for a sheet of composition paper on the table at his elbow, he took a pencil and scribbled these hurried lines:

54

Dear José,—I gave my word not to speak to you, but didn't make any promise about writing. Therefore I can send you this little note. I don't think it's wrong. Anyway, I must do it, because I have missed you so much, and have scarcely been able to sleep at nights for thinking of you.

José, you are working much too hard; please do take it easier. I wish I could help you. You remember you said I was a big help when we did the planting and pruned off the tamarisks. That was great fun.

If your back is stiff get Maria to rub you with the goose-grease, like you told me. Although I can't work, I still do the exercises you showed me and am stronger than ever. Maybe I will be a pelota *player too one day. Write by return and tell me how you feel.*

PS. Did old Pedro and the little five enjoy the trout?

PPS. I hope you are missing me too.

When he had finished Nicholas folded the paper many times into a tight, compact cube. Glancing round carefully to make sure that he was not spied upon from the windows of the villa, he waited until José trundled slowly past him, then, with a fast-beating pulse, threw this missile into the loaded wheelbarrow. It was a good shot. The paper landed between two stones and lodged there safely.

If José was surprised he gave no sign, but continued heavily towards the dump of rocks. Perhaps he had observed nothing, or, worse still, meant to take no notice of the message. The little boy's heart sank, then bounded again as he saw José, before tumbling out the stones, calmly retrieve the paper, conceal it in his palm, then move towards the shelter of the potting shed. Every other journey he would go to the shed to take a drink of water from the wicker-encased stone jar which he kept there, in the cool darkness. But on this occasion he remained out of sight somewhat longer, and when he emerged the first thing Nicholas saw, with a little start, was a yellow stub of pencil, glowing like a crocus, behind his ear.

55

Steadily José plodded back, his expression unchanged, still fixed and set. A faint shiver of doubt contracted the little boy's skin. Then, as the gardener drew abreast, suddenly he smiled, his own familiar, gentle smile, which lit up all his sweat-streaked face and warmed Nicholas by its radiance. At the same time, with a swift motion of his well-trained wrist, almost unseen, he flicked the paper back into Nicholas' lap. The next instant he had disappeared behind the myrtle hedge.

Nicholas drew a deep, joyful breath and after a long minute during which he lay quite still, savouring to the full that sweet smile, which reopened and restored the friendship he had fancied lost, he took the paper from the rug which covered his knees, and slowly unrolled it. There, written roundly, a little untidily, by the thick lead pencil stub, was José's answer:

Amigo mio,—You have more brains than José to think of such cleverness. Write more, for surely it offends nobody. This work is nothing. You know that I am strong as an Andalusian donkey—they are the strongest. Anyhow, I shall take a good rest when I go to the Arengo to fish on Sunday. I wish you might come. The five sisters are well, praise be to God, and old Pedro ate hugely of the trout. Did you truly miss me, little one? That gives me a new heart.

José.

For a full minute Nicholas shut his eyes tight, as though to fix upon the screen of his sight these blessed words. José had not forgotten him. All his being responded to that happy thought in a kind of golden glow. Suddenly he laughed out loud and, sitting erect, snatched up his pencil.

How can you be an Andalusian donkey when you are the best pelota *player in San Jorge? Also the nicest friend I ever had. I've never had a friend before, so that is no great compliment. Ha! Ha! Why don't you oil that old axle? It makes a*

56

horrible squeak. I don't mind, though; it sounds like music to me because it means that you are near. I can't stop laughing, I am so happy.

Nicholas.

Into the wheelbarrow went the paper; then some moments later, it flew back to the rug.

I allow the axle to squeak so that everyone shall know that the lazy gardener is at work. But if you like music one day I will play my clarionet for you. The Catalan tunes would make you skip and jump. Ta-ra, ta-ra, te-da, boom, boom. We do not need to speak that way either. Also we could play ball in silence. You see I am not so stupid.

José the Donkey.

Then again:

If you must be a donkey, then I shall be a flea. Then I can be with you without being seen. And jump as high as you like. But I assure you if you cease to be my friend I shall bite you very hard.

Nicco the Flea.

Next time, as he passed, José did not smile and, opening the paper, Nicholas read:

Pray be careful, little amigo. Garcia is standing in the patio. He has seen nothing, but it is better we write no more until to-morrow. I am thinking of you.

José.

The boy stiffened imperceptibly, like one of these delicate sea plants which, at the first sign of danger, arrest the soft movement of their fronds before withdrawing them. With due caution, he stuffed the paper inside his shirt. A more correct technique—he knew from the books he had read—

57

would be to chew the sheet and swallow it. But it was much too large for that and would have made him sick. Besides, he wished, with all his heart, to keep it. Resting there, his eyes, slightly parted, sheltered by his drooping lids, he was conscious of the caress of the stiff edges of the page, rough and a little sharp upon his skin, moving with his breathing, and with the tender beating of his heart.

EIGHT

AND NOW, OBSERVING José at his appointed task, plodding backwards and forwards, completely silent, much thinner than before, the Consul drew in a sibilant breath of satisfaction. A pity, perhaps, that the rockery was almost completed. Yet, with a grim smile, he reflected that other horticultural operations could be devised, solid and creative works, on a scale calculated to strain the sinews and maintain the limbs in active motion. He would not rest until he had tamed this upstart and rebellious spirit.

At the same time, as his hostility towards the Catalan youth intensified, Brande was aware, within himself, of an exceptional sense of well-being. In his recent years he had never felt better, more fully in possession of all his physical and mental qualities—in short, more intensely alive. He liked warm weather, with its expansive glow, and was suited by the vigorous sunshine of this ardent spring. His office, unworthy of him though it might be, was at last running smoothly; his manuscript on Malbranche advanced in the final stages of revision.

But Brande's deepest gratification came from the manner in which Nicholas had responded to his authority. After those first few days of peevish dejection, he had thrown off his sulks, and 'come round' like a loving and obedient child. Lately, indeed, he had displayed much brightness and gaiety, with fits of gleeful laughter which, although they caused his father to raise a moderating finger, were sure evidence that the disquieting affair had passed completely from his mind.

Ah, it was good to feel the pulse of life, to be filled with this sense of mastery, of potent strength, almost, one might say, of rejuvenation. A new optimism towards the future stirred his blood and made his narrow nostrils dilate. Could it be, at last, that Fortune was about to cease to frown on him, perhaps even to favour him with her smile?

On Saturday afternoon, towards five o'clock, in the warm glow of the sunset he set out with a brisk step to walk to the Consulate. It was a holiday—at least, before his arrival at San Jorge, it had been so regarded, in a loose and somewhat lazy style. But recently, with his passion for efficiency, he had insisted that one member of the staff remain on duty at the office. To-day he had been obliged to let Burton off— Alvin had planned to go picnicking to Huesca with his wife and the Alcade's children, a familiarity which, incidentally, the Consul did not altogether approve—but Fernando, the senior clerk, had been instructed to remain at his post.

It was, indeed, to reassure himself upon this point that Brande chose to call in at the Consulate at this hour. At the same time he meant to look through the mail, which no one was allowed to handle but himself, and which came up every weekday from Barcelona on the afternoon train. This late delivery was a great nuisance, but he had already taken it up strongly with the postal authorities, and hoped that the matter would be adjusted to his satisfaction.

This evening, certainly, he was in no mood to complain. Humming under his breath, he let himself in to the office, noting with immediate satisfaction that Fernando was at his desk.

"Well!" he exclaimed, with unusual geniality, "you are holding the fort, Fernando. Anything to report?"

The clerk straightened himself hastily, his eyes half asleep.

"No, *señor*. And the afternoon has been so fine. Such a pity!" He ventured a timid protest. "One might just as well have been on the beach."

"At least you have the satisfaction of having done your duty, Fernando." Brande spoke in mild reproach. "Tell me, has the mail come in?"

"Yes, *señor*; it is in the box. . . . And the carrier remarked that there was a letter with seals . . . from Madrid. But of course I did not touch it."

"Quite right." Brande nodded. "Well . . . you may go now if you wish."

He stood on one side as Fernando jumped up, seized his hat and with a quick bow ran from the office, like a schoolboy released from detention. Then, shaking his head, he went to the mail-box, unlocked it with the Chubb key on the end of his watch chain. And there, stamped with a heavy red seal, was the letter from Madrid.

Immediately, as he took it up in his broad, well-manicured fingers, he experienced a queer, inexplicable premonitory thrill. Whether or not from the movement of his mood, he seemed to sense that this was, for him, a vital communication. Quickly he slit the envelope. And then, indeed, he saw that the news was of the first importance.

The letter was from Leighton Bailey, the Consul-General at Madrid. It stated, briefly, that George Tenney had been taken seriously ill, stricken by a cerebral seizure which, if not actually fatal, must invalid him permanently from the service. It requested Brande to report immediately to the Embassy.

The Consul remained for an instant perfectly still, his chest expanded, his large body throbbing beneath its immobility. Tensely, he read the letter through again. It could mean only one thing—he was to have Tenney's place; the promotion, so long denied him, had come at last.

Only by the greatest effort did Harrington Brande suppress a glad impulse to cry out. His sense of dignity alone restrained him. But at last . . . at last . . . they had recognised his worth. He breathed deeply, head thrown back, eyeballs glistening . . . abandoned to his joy.

Finally, he mastered himself, collected his thoughts, strode through the doorway to the outer hall and, with an agitated

60

touch, consulted the railway timetable which hung by a cord beside the wall telephone. As he had anticipated, the service was execrable. But if Garcia drove him to Barcelona after dinner, he could take the midnight train to Zaragize which connected with a local coach to Valladolid and here, after an hour's wait, could join the Central Castile express which reached Madrid shortly before noon on Sunday. It would, of course, be a frightful journey but, in view of the honour to be conferred on him, he wished at all costs to impress Bailey with his promptness and punctuality.

Through his elation—was he not, above all, a man of method?—his mind became busy with the details of the trip. He would probably be away for about three days. How fortunate to have such a reliable couple in the house—Nicholas would be well taken care of by Magdalena and the excellent Garcia. Naturally, he counted on the Burtons as an official standby, and when he telephoned Alvin—he would do so from the villa—he would request that they keep an eye upon the boy.

At the thought of Nicholas a brighter gleam illumined the Consul's humid eye. What happiness to convey the news to his dear son, to point out the advantages of this great upward step, to dwell upon the pleasures and privileges of life in the Spanish capital, to explain how fine would be their new establishment, how splendid their social and intellectual advantages, to promise visits to the Prado . . . the Palacio Real . . . the pavilions of Buen Retiro . . . and then, best of all, to feel admiration tinging the warm affection of that childish gaze.

At this, Brande could contain himself no longer. He yearned, suddenly, uncontrollably, to be with the boy. Placing the letter in his pocket-book, he locked up the office, and hastened with all speed towards the street.

61

NINE

AT TEN O'CLOCK that night, when Nicholas, in bed, heard
the whine of the departing car, he burrowed nervously beneath the counterpane. Yet he could still see the reflection
of the headlights as they shot out, swept the ceiling of his
room, like the antennae of a great spider, then disappeared.
And in the darkness which followed, blinding and silent,
he could hear the thin loud beating of his heart. He was so
seldom separated from his father that he felt always a wrench,
when, even for a short period, the Consul went away. But
this time, although he had not dared to speak of it, or even
for that matter to admit it to himself, another anxiety intensified his natural disquiet. How could he stand, alone and
unsupported, against Garcia?

His wakefulness was not that restless tossing which used
to trouble him when he was sick, but a kind of silent tensity
that bound him while he lay there, open-eyed and stiff, in the
old dark Spanish house, listening, listening for the return of
the butler with the car. The creak of a dry board relaxing,
as with a sigh, after the arid heat of day, mice pattering
timidly behind the wainscoting, the tremulous tapping of a
mimosa branch upon the window-pane, all the little gentle
sounds of night which so often reassured him, fell unheeded
upon his ears. Midnight struck upon the long clock in the
hall. Had Garcia cut the motor and coasted in silence towards the stables? If so, he was back, in the house; at any
second his padding step might echo, softly and secretly upon
the stairs. Nicholas shivered, chilled by that unreasoning
mistrust of the butler which he could neither control nor
explain.

He must have fallen asleep at last, for he awoke to a bright
new day, with his tray already on the bedside table and
Magdalena opening his shutters with a cheerful clatter.

"I brought you up breakfast for a little treat."

62

He understood her much better now and sat up with an answering smile. He liked Magdalena, despite these periodic moods which came upon her after the noise of quarrelling in the kitchen, and which drew her broad, swollen brow into a corrugation of resentful misery.

"Did Father get his train all right?" he asked, beginning on the glass of orange juice.

"Yes, yes." She nodded. "I am sure."

"I didn't hear the car come back."

She bent to pick up something invisible from the floor. When she spoke her tone was casual, yet she glanced at him sideways, as though estimating the effect of her words:

"Garcia did not return last night. It was so very late. Indeed, I think he will remain in Barcelona for the week-end. He has friends there. And some business to transact."

Wide-eyed, he stared at her, almost unbelieving, overcome by relief, by an inexpressible rush of joy.

"It's all right?" She nodded, still searching with her gaze. "No need to say anything. We manage very well together, you and me."

"Yes, yes," he exclaimed, scarcely trusting his voice.

"Tell me, then, what you like for lunch."

"Oh, anything you please, Magdalena. You're so decent . . ."

"I do for you something special." She nodded, satisfied, making her earrings dance, and, with her broad, strangely battered smile, she straightened his coverlet and went out of the room.

Left alone, Nicholas stretched himself with a groan of pleasure, then rolled about the big bed, overcome by his good luck, hugging the thought of the precious hours he would spend with José, quite undisturbed, without surveillance. . . .

"And to-morrow too!" he shouted to the woolly dog. "Perhaps even Monday!"

Leaping up, he finished his breakfast, while dressing, in little snatches, glancing from time to time through the win-

63

dow towards the myrtle grove where José had already begun his steady round. Then, with commendable control, he sat down at his little writing table and dashed off a few lines.

Dear José,—Father has gone to Madrid for at least three days. Garcia is away also. Isn't it wonderful? I won't be disobedient. No working or talking—but I mean to be with you all the time. Hurrah!

Your own,
Nicco.

A moment later he was beside José, proffering the note, accepting with a breathless smile his friend's answering pantomime of delight.

All that morning they were together. Most of the rocks had now been moved and the work of filling the crevices of this foundation with soil was not too arduous. When José trundled the wheelbarrow, Nicholas trotted at his heels. While he spaded out the soft earth the little boy sat on a stone, watching, with his chin in his hands, waiting for that heart-warming smile which he knew would come to him. Occasionally José made him laugh outrageously by pretending to talk, moving his lips extravagantly but entirely without words, and ending by blowing out his cheeks in a loud, explosive 'pop.'

As the day advanced, however, José's manner became increasingly preoccupied—something important and mysterious was in his mind. Finally, he put aside the spade, sat down, fumbled for his pencil stub and, while Nicholas looked eagerly over his shoulder, moistened the lead and wrote these splendid words:

Why not come fishing with me to-morrow? I can arrange it with Magdalena.

Even as the little boy gasped in startled rapture, José got up and went through the laurel bushes to the back door. Presently Nicholas heard their voices, Magdalena's and the

64

gardener's, in animated conversation, then came laughter, and more pleasant, friendly talk. How good José was at getting on with people! Everyone liked him, Nicholas reflected, except, unfortunately, Garcia and his father. He was certainly a favourite with Magdalena, who rewarded him for emptying her refuse-cans—a duty that was Garcia's—by handing him a hunk of *pastelena* when nobody was looking. But could he win her round now? With straining ears, Nicholas listened. The door had closed, José was now returning, with unhurried step . . . and yes, it was all right, he had done it . . . one look at his friend's face revealed the happy tidings.

Oh joy, oh inexplicable bliss of this sunlit day and of the greater promise of to-morrow. The happy somnolence of the afternoon was imperishable. The sun drew up the colour of the garden, drenched him with its brightness and its fragrance. Valerian, peonies and lilac made even the shadows glow. A swarm of bees hummed about the honeyed trumpets of a purple creeper that hung from the old catalpa tree. The mountains, in the crystal distance, were blue as flashing steel. This feeling, this warmth in his childish heart—he could not grasp its meaning, but wished only to lose himself, with breathless longing, in its innocent radiance.

Next morning, at eight o'clock, a handful of gravel rattled against his shutters. Only lightly asleep, he sprang out of bed, threw on his clothes, all arranged ready to his hand upon a chair, and went bounding downstairs. In the dim hall he found the wicker basket, covered by a white napkin, which Magdalena had packed for him the night before. Seizing it under his arm, he drew back the heavy bolts, tugged the front door open and, rushing out, dazzled by the level sunshine, almost fell into his friend's arms.

José carried two long bamboo rods and a home-made knapsack upon his shoulder and wore, besides his big garden boots, an old *poncho* fashioned of sailcloth. As they set out together along the lane which led to the main road, he made a little smiling sign to Nicholas that they must hurry. And indeed, they were only just in time for, when they reached the corner, a wheezing chatter of ancient machinery fell upon the ears and immediately the Torrido country bus came in sight.

The bus, which jerked to a halt at José's summons, was extremely crowded, but a place was made for them at the back into which they squeezed, amidst much laughter. They were a gay company in this Sunday bus. Many were going to visit relatives at the little hill farms—working men in flat hats and stiff black *boleros* accompanied by their wives, swathed in innumerable petticoats, with coloured hand-kerchiefs bound about their heads and many packages at their feet, bottles of *manzanilla* wrapped in pink paper, wicker baskets of eggs, ripe apricots and pomegranates, fresh-made *quesadilla*. Others, like José, had rods and fishing bags beside them. Some carried queer little cages in which they were going to catch crickets. One, a long lean fellow, a bit of a clown, draped in a great plaid cape, who was eating a sausage with hungry bites, had a gun with a tremendous barrel. An old man with a goatskin of wine was already beginning to make *fiesta*.

José had been recognised at once, received, in fact, with general acclaim, and immediately he was the centre of an animated conversation. The prospects for the next *pelota* game were discussed. Some thought that Jaime, the veteran, should be replaced, but José staunchly supported his partner. Then the goatskin was passed round. Each man raised it up and, throwing back his head, spirited a thin red stream expertly into the deep recesses of his throat. After that, the laughter increased, and many jokes were made, especially against the man with the long gun, who also had a long nose. But the raillery was jovial and goodnatured, and the little boy who had never been allowed to mix with 'common people' could not help reflecting how different it was from what he had believed, how jolly and free. Nor could he altogether suppress the thought of how changed all this would have been had his father been here, how the Consul

66

would have chilled this friendly warmth with his grave and formal presence.

By this time they had left the sandy vineyards and the quiet lowland groves where the docile olives stood in rows, and were amongst the wilder stretches of the Torrida foothills. Slowly, in its lowest gear, the bus began to climb the steeper gradients, passing slower, plodding donkeys jingling with ornament, winding round the shoulders of hills lighted by yellow broom. Every now and then it stopped to allow some of the passengers to descend at a wayside *posada* or a little farm, which, Nicholas decided, was a lucky thing since it gave the old machine a chance to recover its breath. He was very excited now, perched on the edge of the seat, peering through the grey beeches and cork oaks for his first sight of the river. Occasionally, as they went grinding up, higher and higher into the mountains, he glanced at the half-dozen passengers remaining in the bus, all of them anglers, wondering, a little jealously, if there would be space for everyone on the bank. But José, interpreting that look, shook his head gently to indicate that he need not worry. And indeed, at the next village, opposite the inn, all the others got off, with many hearty farewells, leaving the two of them alone.

When the bus restarted José gazed at his companion in a manner peculiarly direct and, with a start of intuition, Nicholas sensed that he was about to break the bond of silence which lay between them.

"Nicco," said José, nodding reassuringly as the little boy drew back. "Yes ... I am speaking to you. Not to do so would be childish. And dangerous too. We are going to the river. I must tell you what to do." He smiled. "I don't want you to fall in. Your father would blame me more for that than for talking. But you ... you need not speak a word."

Wide-eyed, Nicholas stared back at his friend. Suddenly a responsive wave, poignant with affection, overcame him.

"I will speak, José." The words came tumbling hotly out. "If you speak, I'll speak too."

"Well then," said José with a deepening of his gentle smile,

67

"we shall be like men and not like timid children. Also we shall enjoy ourselves much better. Come now, this is where we descend."

He gathered up his rods and knapsack, and helped Nicholas to the front of the bus where, leaning forward, he tapped on the cracked glass partition. As they drew up, he leaped out and the next instant, reaching up a long arm, had his companion beside him. They waved to the driver who looked out of his wooden box to shout "Good luck!" then, as the vehicle lurched away, turned off the dusty road into a meadow overgrown with pale new bracken.

Although the sun shone brilliantly, the air was cool and crisp, spicy with the scent of thyme and resin. Ahead of them were those peaks which from below had appeared to offer themselves but which now, though sharp and clear, seamed with the silver threads of waterfalls, withdrew as they advanced, remained majestic and inaccessible, their grey flanks and hollow cheeks caressed cautiously by the sunlight, yielding to no one and to nothing save where, high, high amidst the naked boulders, the pines had made a retreat in solitude for themselves.

The purity of the light was dazzling. Looking back across his shoulder Nicholas could see on a ridge to the left a tiny village which seemed cut out of air, then, further down, the little square patches of fields and vineyards and, beyond, a different haze which was the sea, so far below him that he felt himself on the summit of the world.

Tramping through the mitred bracken which brushed and tickled his bare knees, Nicholas took a long, full breath of the delicious freshness.

"It's a wonderful day, José."

"Yes," José agreed, with a little twist to his lips. "But I think too bright for fishing. However, we shall see."

They were in a wood now and going downhill through beech trees that grew large and wide apart on rough grassland where some goats were grazing, incurious of their approach. But suddenly they came through this belt into the open, and

68

there, stretching out almost at their feet, was a green valley, with the broad river swirling past an old greystone watermill, and foaming over the dam into a wide pool beyond.

"This is the place," José said in an off-hand voice, yet with secret pride.

"Oh, José!" Nicholas exclaimed. "It's the nicest ever. Why don't the others come here?"

"Too far from the inn." José laughed. "They wish to drink as well as fish."

He set the pace down the path to the mill, hurrying slightly from his own excitement, Nicholas leaping, skipping on his toes, beside him. It was warmer in the valley, and clumps of wild blue irises, with cowslips, yellow as butter, grew on the grassy slopes. The mill, Nicholas could now see, was a ruin, with no roof, beyond a few stark rafters, and a motionless moss-covered wheel, but this merely increased the splendid sense of privacy which lay upon the valley.

On the stone steps of the mill, facing the river, José laid down his gear and began to thread a light line through each of the bamboos. They were the cheapest kind of rods, with wooden reels, but José treated them with loving care, although his fingers trembled with eagerness as he tied on the long gut leaders.

"You like to fish, don't you, José" Nicholas asked.

"Most emphatically, *amigo*," José nodded, blithely. "Don't you?"

"I love it," Nicholas answered. "Only I've never had the chance."

"You will now." José smiled. "Look, Nicco, my friend, you are not yet large enough to throw a fly, so you will fish with bait. . . . Wait now. . . . I shall show you something which the trout are crazy about."

He drew from his knapsack a smooth round tin, removed the lid, and shook into his palm a fat meal maggot which, with solicitude, he baited on the hook. Then, taking Nicholas by the hand, he led him a short way out on the stone dam, seated

69

him comfortably, with his legs dangling, threw the leaded line into the pool and gave him the rod.

"There," he said. "If you feel a bite, pull hard."

"You won't go far away?"

"No, no, *amigo*." He pointed to the broken water above the dam. "Only up there."

At first Nicholas sat stiff and tense, holding the rod tight with both hands, his head giddy with the rush of white water over the weir, a little fearful that he might fall in. Gradually, however, a glow of confidence stole over him. How wonderful it was to be treated as a boy, an ordinary boy, and not as a puny, ailing child. Carefully, so as not to lose his balance, he turned his head and looked upstream where, knee-deep in the foaming current, José stood working his long rod, the line curving in a graceful sweep as it rose and fell in the clear air. Once he thought he saw a trout leap high in the rapids. He could not tell. The crumbling mortar on the wall was warm beneath him. Ferns were growing from the cracks, and a rough grey lichen encrusted the old stones.

Suddenly he started. He had not felt the trout bite, but all at once his rod had come alive, bending and quivering in a lively arc, imparting to him from beneath the surface of the pool a delirious sense of weight and motion.

"I've got one," he gasped, turning white to the lips. Instinctively, in a flurry of panic, he gazed towards José, now with his back turned about a hundred yards away, separated by a roaring waste of water. Impossible to call for help. He must do it all himself. Desperately, he clung to the rod while the clumsy wooden reel whirred and bumped against his chest. The trout was fighting like mad, tearing about in wild rushes in the foamy cataract, then burrowing deep down towards the sandy bottom, as though at any second it might break loose. Suddenly it jumped clean out of the water, landing back with a smack, which brought the little boy's heart into his throat.

"Oh, what a beauty," he panted to himself. "Oh, please God, don't let him get away."

Carefully, carefully, he began to wind up the reel. The trout was tiring now. Nicholas could see the thick, thrilling curve of its speckled body just beneath the surface. Trembling all over, he got to his feet and stumbled back along the dam to the bank which, a few paces downstream, sloped gently into the pool. Here, winding in still more, he towed the trout towards the shallows, then, with a final convulsive tug, brought it safely to the shingle.

He had done it, he had caught this splendid trout all by himself. His first impulse was to run feverishly to José, to tell him the great news. But a new sense of self-mastery withheld him. Steeling himself, he knelt and unhooked the trout, stilled it with a hard bang on the head, then laid it amongst some ferns in the shadow of the mill steps. A moment later he was back on the dam, his line rebaited, waiting, with sparkling eyes, for the next trout to strike.

When José came down after one o'clock, Nicholas had two more fish neatly placed beside the first, not quite so large perhaps, but good trout all the same.

"Any luck?" asked José.

Then the little boy's restraint broke down. He wound in his line, rushed to the bank and, seizing José by the arm, dragged him bodily towards his catch.

"Look, José, look! Aren't they beauties? I got the biggest first. Oh, it was tremendous! I was scared to death. But I did it. Took the hook out and everything. I tell you I've never had such fun in all my life. But I'm sorry, José. I quite forgot. Did you get any?"

It turned out that José had four in his knapsack, but he did not make a show of them. He seemed too happy at Nicholas' success. His trousers were wringing wet, and his face streaked with sweat.

"Now," he smiled, "it is time for us to eat. I hope your appetite is as great as mine."

He sat down on the steps, took some coarse bread, a wedge of cheese wrapped in newspaper, and a raw onion from his knapsack, then, opening his big clasp-knife with a flourish,

71

made a quick sign of the Cross. Nicholas, recollecting he had eaten no breakfast, suddenly discovered that he was starving. He took his place beside José and uncovered the wicker basket, shamed a little by the spotless white napkin, and by all the good things Magdalena had packed for him—the hard-boiled eggs and cold chicken, with rolls and butter, fresh fruits, and a section of comb honey—yet rejoicing, too, that he would be able to offer them to his dear friend.

At first José refused to touch these unusual delicacies but, seeing the hurt disappointment in Nicholas's eyes, he laughed a little awkwardly, and gave in, suggesting that they share their food. It was a good meal, eaten in the warm sun, close to the earth, with the sound of the river in their ears. Nicholas found the black bread and onion much tastier than he had expected and he could see, from the manner in which he polished the bone with his white teeth, that José enjoyed the chicken. Every now and then he cast glances at his trout, lying cool in the fern. They talked about fishing and José explained where the trout lay at various seasons of the year, sometimes in fast water, sometimes in slack, and how one must tempt them with the proper lure, a tiny fly in the dry weather, a spinning minnow in the flood. He told of past expeditions, of setting nightlines, and how once he had hooked a huge cannibal pike, the grandfather of them all, played him for an hour, then lost him in the weeds.

Nicholas could have listened to this entrancing talk for ever, but José, discerning with a shrewd glance signs of tiredness in the child's face, suddenly stood up.

"Mustn't forget that you rose very early, *amigo*. It is time for your *siesta*."

Waving aside all protests, he cut an armful of the soft bracken with his knife, spread this in the shadow of the mill, and covered it with his *poncho*.

"There," he said. "See if it is comfortable . . . little one who pretends to be sick."

Obediently, Nicholas stretched out his limbs, which were stinging and glowing with healthy tiredness. Placing his

72

hands under his head, he watched José go to the river, wash the plates and cutlery, and replace them in Magdalena's basket. Then he saw him pluck fresh fern and some stalks of wild mint and pack in the trout as well. The beech trees and the cork oaks had taken on their midday silver glitter. Languor and stillness enclosed the valley. A bird called lazily in the golden air. The sound was warm and drowsy. He closed his eyes.

When José came back, Nicholas, flat on his back, was fast asleep. And as he gazed at that supine form, so fragile and defenceless, José, who had meant to take his rod and try the streams below the weir, abruptly changed his mind. Instead, as though under a strange compulsion, he settled down, silently, on the ground, close to the little boy, while his dark, gentle eyes, made darker by a deep compassion, remained fixed upon that unconscious face, a trifle pale beneath its freckles, the soft cheeks shadowed by long curly lashes, the milky teeth showing beneath the short upper lip.

José's upbringing had been hard. When his father died he was only twelve, and a few months later he was taken from school and sent to work in the fields. He had known poverty, exacting labour, the grinding anxiety of the breadwinner. All this had made him resolute and self-contained: he was no easy prey for idle fancies or tenuous emotions. Moreover, his cheerful disposition and his prowess at *pelota* had made him a universal favourite, given him many friends. And he had, of course, his mother, the five sisters, even old Pedro—every one of whom he dutifully loved. Yet all this was nothing beside this new, melting affection for this little boy, which, soft as a southern air, had sprung from he knew not where, filling him with tenderness, and with a strange protective pity. He could not account for it. He only knew that it made his heart sing.

José's mind, although alert, was not especially subtle, yet he read, clear as day, the evidence that was written upon these nervous features which flickered, even now, in sleep. The Consul's possessive love, raising an impassable barrier

73

between Nicholas and the world, his dread of illness that, by its fads and fussiness, had reduced the child to a state of chronic invalidism, his morbid jealousy, so exhausting to the youthful spirit, his moods and rages, inflicted continually, his stupid pride. . . . José instinctively surmised them all and, with his whole soul, he wished that he might free this unsuspecting victim and restore him unburdened to a natural life.

The sun had begun to sink towards the high rim of the hills when Nicholas opened his eyes.

"Goodness. I've been asleep." He caught sight of the river and abruptly sat up. "Are we going to fish some more?"

José directed a speculative glance towards the sky, turning to daffodil against the peaks, now colder than before, blue as the shadows upon snow.

"I think, *amigo*, that it is time for us to leave."

"Oh, José . . . !"

Smiling, José shook his head and laid his hand lightly on Nicholas' shoulder.

"We must go to meet the bus. Wouldn't do to miss it. But don't worry, Nicco. We shall come again."

To come again, here, to this lovely spot, with his dear friend—a radiant satisfaction came into the boy's eyes. He jumped to his feet with an irrepressible shout.

They wound the reels, detached the casts, and put away the tackle. They picked up their fish. Nicholas insisted on carrying his own. Then they went up the hill, together.

TEN

IT WAS RATHER late, almost nine o'clock that evening, when Nicholas approached the Casa Breza, but so high were his spirits he felt quite undaunted by the darkness. The journey in the crowded bus had been hilarious, with much laughter and singing—high-pitched Catalan singing—filled

74

with queer lifts and cadences, with quivering 'arrows' of harmony, in which, to his own surprise, he had actually joined. He had been made much of, praised for his catch, especially by the man with the long nose, who had shot nothing, and in general treated like a brave and hardy boy. Flushed with his success, he had refused José's offer to get off the bus and escort him to the villa entrance.

So here he was, quite alone, marching up towards the *patio* steps, scarcely afraid at all of the shadows which lurked and rustled in the ilex trees. The first thing he meant to do was to go into the kitchen, display his trout to Magdalena, and ask her to cook them for his breakfast. He opened the front door, then paused, confronted by the darkness of the hall. Goodness! how dark it was, like a great black cave. Magdalena had forgotten to light the crystal gasolier which hung suspended by a metal chain from the high roof. Guided by a glimmer of starlight from behind him, he advanced a few cautious paces with outstretched hands. Suddenly a start passed over all his body. In the pantry on the left he heard sounds of a violent argument, a man's voice, dull and thickened, and a woman's, sharp with fear—it was Garcia and Magdalena.

He had never expected that the butler would have returned; his blood seemed to stop circulating in his veins, all his gaiety, his new assurance, was gone. He turned cautiously on tiptoe, trying to avoid the squeaky boards, when, all at once, a gust from the sea caught the front door, which still remained half open, and slammed it shut with shattering force.

Plunged again in complete darkness, Nicholas stood stockstill, as if stunned by the reverberating echoes which crashed about the lofty hall. At the same moment a flood of light dazzled his eyes, and Garcia came out of the pantry holding up an Argand lamp. Always, for the child, there was something dismaying in that gliding figure, but now especially, magnified by the blinding glare, swaying a little as it advanced, yet planting the feet with particular care, it was more fearful than ever before. Unable to resist, Nicholas felt him-

75

self caught by the hand and drawn into the pantry where his dilated pupils focused in blurred fashion on the form of Magdalena, sullen and swollen-eyed, seated at the white enamel table, on which stood the remnants of a meal and a bottle of *aguardiente*, almost empty.

"The little master has returned." Garcia spoke with frightening slowness, using his words with that same studious care. His smooth face was pale as bone and his mouth hung down, livid as a wound. "Where has the little master been?"

Nicholas could not find his tongue, nor could he move his terror-stricken gaze from that awful, sneering face. At last he gasped out:

"Fishing!"

"Fishing," repeated the butler in an indescribable tone. "Then where are the fish?"

Speechless, Nicholas held out the basket which he still clutched tight in his shaking hand. Garcia took it slowly; then with a sudden jerk threw the contents upon the table. Two of the trout shot across and fell upon the floor. The third, the smallest, remained upon the enamelled surface, its spine curled up, looking somehow pitiful and mean.

"Bah!" Garcia sneered. "That is no way to bring me fish ... unclean and unprepared."

While Nicholas watched, rooted with fear, the butler seized the bread knife from the platter and with a single stroke struck off the little trout's head. A thin trickle of pink blood oozed across the white table.

"No one will treat me like a scullion," he exclaimed, staring at the boy. "You understand?"

"Yes," stammered Nicholas, seeing that an answer was demanded of him.

Garcia smiled, without moving his lips.

"Why do you shiver, little master? Because you are surprised to find me here? Don't you know I come and go exactly as I please?"

"Oh, yes ... of course," whispered Nicholas, convulsively.

"It is well that you agree." The butler drew himself up in

76

menacing fashion. "People who are against me I stamp out like an insect."

Magdalena, rocking herself to and fro, began groaning under her breath:

"Be quiet, madman . . . be quiet . . . for God's sake be quiet."

Garcia took no notice of her whatsoever. He was still caressing the handle of the knife. Nicholas, pale as death, could see the cloudy film slide, like dirty oil, over his opaque eyes, as in a soft voice, he repeated:

"Like an insect. . . . Some day I am going to tell you of all the things I have done. I promised you before . . . perhaps you have forgotten. Never mind. The day will come when you will believe me. Meantime, you must not be against me. No spying or interference. You know that I never sleep. . . . I am always about . . . in the passages . . . watching in your room."

"No . . . no." The terrified cry was inarticulate, it stuck in the child's throat, hung weakly suspended in the air.

Again the butler smiled, as though gratified, and took a slow, balanced step nearer to Nicholas. The weight of these crazy, melancholy eyes, burning in the pallid face, filled the child with horror and disgust. His very being seemed poisoned at the source. Desperately, he tried to draw back, but his body no longer obeyed him.

"Yes," murmured Garcia. "You are a wretched little boy. But there are many things I can teach you. . . . I can teach you the great mystery." He broke off, his gaze suddenly fixed and distant, then continued, in a low tone, as though speaking to himself: "The joy of forgetfulness . . . the sea of oblivion . . . those tremendous voices. . . ."

With an irrepressible start, her brow contorted, Magdalena straightened herself.

"Be silent," she shouted hoarsely. "You drunken swine . . . you crazy, drunken devil. . . ."

Wrenched from his dream, Garcia turned towards her and, as she made to rise, he struck her in the face with his left hand.

77

It was not a hard blow, but the shock of it seemed to liberate the boy's paralysed muscles, gave to him the power of flight. With a shrill, high whimper, which was lost in Magdalena's wailing, he spun round and stumbled from the pantry. Up the staircase he went, falling down, picking himself up again, feeling no hurt, feeling nothing but the overpowering desire to escape.

At last he was in his room. He banged the door shut and, with numb fingers, turned the big key. Then he shot the bolt in the door which communicated with his father's bedroom. The shutters were already closed. Trembling all over, his heart fluttering like a bird against the cage of his ribs, he stood in the darkness, in the centre of the room. He was afraid to light the gas. He wanted only to hide. Kicking off his shoes, he crept towards the bed and, still wearing his clothes, buried himself beneath the blankets. Yet even here he could still see Garcia as he had advanced towards him, with that expression on his face which seemed to shatter his childish universe, and the stab of shame and panic that went through him was so painful it brought scalding tears to his eyes. Oh, if only José, dear José, had been there to protect him! At the thought of José he wept as he had never wept before.

That long, that endless night, would he ever forget it? The lamentations of Magdalena, ascending from below, the shouting, bursts of louder quarrelling, the smash of a breaking bottle, laughter, unbelievable laughter, the sounds of further blows. And then the silence, the stealthy, succeeding silence, worse by far than any tumult, the silence suffused by the anguish of uncertainty, of imagined and unidentifiable movements. What, oh, what was that? Was he dreaming or awake? Had he really locked the door? He dared not move to reassure himself, but, bathed in an icy sweat which soaked his pillow, he lay there, wide-eyed and motionless, lost in a dreadful vertigo.

At last, when hope had almost gone, he saw faint streaks of dawn beneath the shutters. Then, for a little while, he may have drowsed. When consciousness returned he lay on his

78

side, listening again. Not a sound, not a movement stirring in the house. He found courage to get up, to open a shutter. And there—oh, relief unbelievable—he saw José in the garden, working in his singlet, hoeing the petunia bed with sane and easy strokes, the wheelbarrow and watering can beside him, in the clear golden light of another day.

There was no need to dress. Unlocking the door, he flew downstairs, rushed out along the gravel path and hurled himself upon his friend.

"Oh, José . . . José . . ." For a long time he could do no more than repeat that name, but gradually, in a broken manner, but without crying, he unburdened his overloaded heart.

Seated on the wheelbarrow, José heard him without a word, not looking at him, in fact, except for a few swift, half-frowning glances. When Nicholas had finished, he seemed to ponder for a moment; then he stood up. Through his assumed cheerfulness a harder maturity had settled upon his face.

"You must have some food, Nicco. Wait here while I see about it."

He walked slowly but resolutely past the bushes to the back door, then, after only a brief interval, he returned.

"Magdalena has made your breakfast, *amigo*. Do not worry about Garcia. He is still asleep." He paused. "I shall be near."

For no one but José would Nicholas have re-entered the house. He obeyed without a word. In the dining-room Magdalena gave him breakfast which was as usual, except that the toast was burnt. She moved with a sluggish, apathetic tread; her hair at the back was dishevelled and her face more puffy than ever. He could smell the strong taint of brandy still on her breath. She paid no heed to him at all until he had gulped down the last of his milk, then, standing by the pantry door, hands folded limply beneath her short black apron, she turned upon him her dull yet harassed eye.

"Garcia meant no harm last night. He had taken too much *aguardiente*. It will not happen again."

He stared at her in silence.

79

"You are a good boy," she went on. "You will not speak of it to Señor Brande."

"Not unless I have to," he answered in a strained and husky voice.

"Very well." She shrugged listlessly. "Now you must go and wash."

Nicholas went upstairs, washed hurriedly, brushed his teeth, and changed his shirt. After that, he felt better, for his skin had been stiff and grubby, yet it was a wan and wistful face which returned his gaze from the mirror above his chest of drawers. He felt, not like himself, but like a strange boy, and could not bear to remain longer in this room which, once his cherished retreat, was now altered too, spoiled by the horror of last night, stained and sinister. He ran into the garden again.

All the forenoon he spent close beside José, scarcely talking at all, taking no interest in the work, but throwing, from time to time, across his shoulder, a quick and furtive glance towards the pantry window which stood there, in the façade of the villa, like a blank picture frame, ready to receive that smooth and hateful countenance. José did not speak much either, and it was plain, from his bent brows and compressed lips, that he was not disposed to treat the situation lightly, and was, perhaps, concerned by the personal problem which it presented. He, too, gazed occasionally towards the house.

At one o'clock there was still no sign of the butler. When Magdalena signed that his lunch was prepared Nicholas would have preferred not to go in, but José's expression, which seemed to demand from him an equal firmness, permitted no evasion. He noticed, however, that while he was indoors his friend remained beside the dining-room window. And, indeed, even when he rejoined him, José kept quite close to the villa, weeding the gravel circle, on his hands and knees, silent and watchful.

At three o'clock the front door opened and Garcia came out on the portico, bare-headed, wearing only a shirt and trousers, his bare feet thrust into rope-soled *alpargatas*. At the

80

sight of his enemy, Nicholas nearly jumped from his skin. The man was pallid and sullen, and looked only half awake, with bistre shadows circling his eyes, and on his brow that brand of unspeakable malevolence. Shuffling forward, he placed an arm round one of the columns of the porch and, supporting himself, drew in short gulps of air. By this time José had risen quietly to his feet and as Garcia half turned, his gaze fell upon the gardener and Nicholas.

He did not stir, nor did José, and while they stood motionless, staring at each other, Nicholas could feel, with a tightening of all his nerves, the silent battle waged between them. For at least a minute the duel continued. Not a word was spoken. Then the butler's eyes fell, he muttered something under his breath, spat, like a snake extruding its venom, then swung off the portico in the direction of the coach-house. A moment later Nicholas could hear him beginning to hose the car.

The little boy turned towards his protector, but José, if he had been the victor in this contest of wills, showed little evidence of triumph. On the contrary, his forehead was furrowed, more darkly thoughtful than before. Abruptly he demanded:

"*Amigo*, will your father return to-day?"

"Oh, no. He won't come till to-morrow at the earliest."

"Then do you wish to stay here, in the house, to-night?"

"Oh, no, no, José. Anything but that. You don't want me to, do you?"

There was a pause. José looked at the ground, then at Nicholas, with that mingling of affection and perplexity.

"It is hard for me, Nicco. I don't like to make trouble for myself. Yet I cannot . . . no, I cannot leave you here with that *picaro*."

"Oh, thank you, thank you, José."

But José, for once, was not responsive; indeed, his manner was quite abrupt as he replied:

"Enough. No more work for to-day. You are coming home with me."

ELEVEN

NICHOLAS HAD NO idea where José lived. It was enough that he should be with him now, walking to the town, away from Garcia and the Casa Breza. And in the swift reversal of his mood, all that he had suffered was momentarily forgotten. He chattered a little giddily, in fact, on all sorts of topics, breaking off to point to peculiar objects which caught his eye: a black-and-yellow bird, an odd flower by the roadside, the tawny sail of a *barca* gleaming far out in the bay. José, however, seemed occupied with his own thoughts. As they entered the Plaza, he drew up at the broad flight of steps leading to the pink stucco church.

"Remain here a moment, Nicco."

"Where are you going?"

"Somewhere I do not go often." The corner of José's mouth lifted. "But I think it pretty smart for me to go today."

"I'll come with you."

José hesitated; then, shrugging his shoulders, he led the way with a rather bad grace up the long flight of worn, shallow steps.

The church appeared enormous to Nicholas, filled with a lofty darkness and with a strange, musky smell. The roof swept up in painted bulges, and at the sides were many dark alcoves where candles burned and smoked. Towards one of these José advanced and, signing himself, knelt down with his head inclined in a sudden tensity of posture before a glass case, loaded with gilt hearts, in which, against a red velvet hanging, stood a beautiful little figure, half woman, half child, dressed in blue—all real clothes, Nicholas could see— with a tiny gold, jewelled crown upon her head. Only for a few seconds did José kneel, then, advancing, he dropped a coin in the box and lit a candle in the rack of red glass cups.

Outside, Nicholas perceived that José had no wish to talk about this incident, yet he sensed, confusedly, that it was he who, in some manner, had occasioned it. And suddenly he declared:

"I will pay for the candle, José."

He could not understand why his friend burst out laughing, then patted him consolingly upon the back.

They were now in the network of narrow streets, north of the Plaza, which Nicholas had traversed with his father on the way to the *pelota* court. And presently they turned out of an alleyway on to the Calle Corriente, a long, poor thoroughfare fronting the river which at this point received the effluent from the public wash-house. Tall, dilapidated tenements of a soft sienna shade ran along the other side of the street. Bedding hung from the open windows. Somewhere a mandoline string was plucked, vibrated in the air. A team of donkeys drank from a metal trough while their driver took his ease stretched, barefooted, upon the low river wall. On the broken pavement, covered with chalk marks, many children were playing strange games with a silent and secret intensity. The scene, the presence of these children, dismayed Nicholas slightly, and he glanced up inquiringly at his friend. But José, his eye arrested by the figure of a woman, short and middle-aged, bowed under a large bundle wrapped in a white sheet, just ahead of them, had hastened his pace.

"There is my mother, Nicco. . . ." He called out: "Maria . . . Maria Santero."

The next minute they caught her up; José took over the bundle of washing, and, speaking rapidly into her ear, set out to explain the situation. Nicholas saw that it was not easy. Across the worn, swarthy features, made darker by the well-marked eyebrows and tight-drawn black hair, there flickered emotions of surprise, uncertainty, even fear. But before anything more could be said they had all turned into a narrow passage and were climbing an endless stone stair between chocolate-coloured walls. At the very top José opened a narrow door with his free hand.

83

"Hey, Nicco," he exclaimed cheerfully. "This is our palace. Only two rooms. But the best view in town."

They entered a queer, low-ceilinged room, a combination of kitchen and parlour, with an iron cooking stove at one end and a faded yellow plush settee at the other. A varnished table laid for supper and chairs of the same light wood crowded together in the centre of the wooden floor. The light green walls were hung with photographs in shell-encrusted frames, with a case of stuffed humming-birds, another of butterflies, a pair of *pelota* baskets, a sporting calendar, and several coloured sacred pictures. By the window, on a low stool, a very old man was seated, wearing a round black *capillo* and knitting with long bone needles, while, busy at the stove, stirring a steaming iron pot, stood a dark-eyed, sturdy-bosomed little girl of about twelve.

"Pedro . . . and Paquita," José explained to Nicholas as he slid the bundle from his shoulder. "Where are the others?"

"Not back from school," Paquita answered, still stirring the pot, her astounded gaze fixed upon Nicholas. "You are early."

"Perhaps so," said José carelessly.

Maria, the mother, had not taken off her shawl. Nor had she lost her troubled air. She murmured to José.

"Come, my son. We must speak together."

They went into the other room.

No sooner had they disappeared than Nicholas heard the sound of clattering footsteps on the stairs, then the door opened, and four other little girls, wearing home-made holland pinafores, burst into the room, each carrying a dog-eared book of tables, a catechism, a small white square of sewing.

Nicholas went hot and cold all over. Never in all his life had he been in such close contact with so many small girls at the same time. Rocking on his heels, not knowing what to say, he frowned at the butterflies, feeling himself turn a dusky red. Surprisingly, the old man saved him.

"What is your name, young *señor*?"

84

"Nicholas."

"These are José's other sisters. Juana, the youngest, who is five, the good Luisa, aged seven, then clever Elena, not yet nine, and finally Bianca, the wicked one, two years younger than Paquita."

They all crowded round Nicholas without the slightest embarrassment, inspecting him with open curiosity, fingering his tie, his braces, his bootlaces, bombarding him with questions.

"Whence do you come, strange boy?"

"What is the purpose of your visit?"

"In the name of God, who are you?"

The last interrogation, thrown out by the wicked Bianca, seemed most worthy of his notice.

"I am the son of Mr. Harrington Brande. . . ." He spoke rather stiffly. "United States Consul in Spain."

"Eh . . . eh!" Luisa exclaimed with awe. "The young *señor* Americano. Son of José's master!"

They drew back slightly, in a respectful manner, and began to talk in low voices amongst themselves. Nicholas's face got redder than ever, for of course they were speaking of him. However, at that point, José and his mother returned to the living-room and he could see from their faces, though Maria still seemed faintly troubled, that everything was arranged.

"Come now . . . supper for everyone." Maria's embattled expression relaxed further, and she smiled at him in a special kind of way. "I hope you like *olla podrida*, Nicholas."

They sat down at the table and Maria worked slowly round, holding the big pot in her white, sodden hand—even the nails were bleached from washing—ladling a portion of stew on to everyone's plate. José, at the head of the table, cut thick slices of the black bread which Nicholas had tasted at the river—how long ago, how far away that seemed!—then Luisa, 'the good one,' said grace and everyone began to eat.

There was neither sauce nor wine, and for butter they

85

used olive oil spread thinly on the dark bread. The meat in the stew was dark and stringy, certainly of the cheapest quality, and not plentiful either, yet it was so savoury, mixed with onion and the dark red flakes of pimento, that Nicholas had seldom tasted so good a dish.

Maria, he noticed, took a very modest helping for herself, and Pedro, with the retiring air of one who knows his position, held up his hand lest he be given too much. Only José, the real man of the house, was offered a second portion.

Emulating the others, Nicholas used his last crust to polish off his plate. Then Paquita rose, took a stoneware jug from the stove and poured out for each person a scalding cup of coffee. This shocked Nicholas somewhat, for he knew that such a beverage was not suitable for children. However, not for the world would he be different from the others: he sipped the gritty brew, which tasted of burnt grain, without making a wry face.

With the coffee, conversation began, and to the Consul's son—used to the long, sepulchral silences which vibrated across the polished mahogany at home, like a tuning fork within a tomb—it seemed quite wonderful that everyone at this table should talk at once. The children, whose meagre little bodies contained a world of animation, recounted their doings at school with flashing, sidelong glances towards the visitor; Maria was describing to Paquita a dress which she had seen in a shop window in the arcade—a dress of green velvet with claret sleeves—oh, by the bones of Saint Pilar, a *magnifico* dress; while José, at ease, his coat hung on the back of his chair, discussed with Pedro the chances of San Jorge in their return match against Huesca. And presently, indeed, despite his shyness, Nicholas was drawn into this conversation by his friend.

"What is your opinion, *amigo mio*?"

Nicholas took a deep breath.

"If you play as you did last time, you are sure to win." He faltered, but valiantly went on to express a thought which

86

had long been in his mind. "You ought to play in a big city, José. And be paid a lot of money."

José showed his teeth in a wide smile.

"I am not good enough for a big city. Besides, I should stifle to death there. I need the country, Nicco, with much fresh air and fine fishing."

"We Santeros have always played *pelota*. But only for sport," remarked Pedro in his gentle voice. "José's father was a famous player . . . that is his photograph." He pointed to the likeness of a thickset man with a curled moustache, wearing the *cresta*. "And I . . . even I was in my humble way a performer."

"You were the best of us all, old Pedro," José protested. "Some time you must tell Nicco about your match with Zarossa."

The old man smiled in a pleased fashion.

"Shall you go to practice this evening?" he asked presently. "Jaime sent word that he would be there."

But José, without hesitation, shook his head. And a warm wave of happiness passed over Nicholas as his friend answered:

"To-night I shall remain with Nicco. Hey! Flock of chattering magpies! What about a hand of *estallido*? We must show this great Americano that we are smarter than he thinks."

A chorus of approval greeted this suggestion. Bianca ran to the dresser and brought out a worn pack of cards. The table was quickly cleared and, with the exception of Maria who said she must sort out and mend some linen, the entire party gave themselves up to the game.

It was a good game which, once Nicholas grasped the simple rules, went faster and faster with a fine slapping down of cards, squeals of excitement from Juana, sudden shouts of laughter. From outside, through the open window, came the steady hum of the town, the tramp of promenaders by the river, newsboys calling aloud the evening *Gaceta*, the rumble

87

of cartwheels, a chime of bells. Lights sprang out below, sparkling necklaces stretched along the streets, at the Teatro a sign switched on and off. This surrounding brightness, the reassuring sense of human life everywhere about him, the friendly gaiety within the room, all had their due effect on Nicholas. The nightmare shadows which lay in wait for him retreated further, further, until they ceased almost to exist. How could it be that in this mean dwelling, which bore everywhere the stamp of poverty, after a meal that barely satisfied his need, amongst these ordinary working people, he was happy and at ease? He did not pause to reason, but, seizing the opportunity, drank deeply of his joy. His eyes glittered, his laughter rang more shrilly, as he snatched and scrambled for the cards.

They played much later than he could have believed, but towards nine o'clock, at the conclusion of a hand, Maria put down her sewing and rose from her seat by the window.

"Perhaps that is the finish?" she suggested mildly. "I think it is time for bed."

Caught unawares, in the middle of a little shout, Nicholas remained with his mouth wide open, gazing at her foolishly, arrested by an awful, unconsidered difficulty. How should they all sleep in the cramped space of this tiny house? It was impossible. Would they turn him out, then? Return him, at this hour, to the Casa Breza?

The look on his face was so transparent it made José laugh.

"Do not worry, Nicco. You are the worst boy to worry I ever knew. It is quite easy. See!" He lay back in his chair, made a long arm, and threw open the inner door. "All the women sleep in there."

Staring into the other room, Nicholas perceived that it was occupied, almost entirely, by two large brass-mounted beds. Yes, he reflected, still incredulous, it might perhaps be possible.

"But what about us?" he exclaimed suddenly.

José pointed to Maria who, behind the stove, had pulled aside a tasselled cotton curtain, revealing a square recess in the wall occupied by a box-bed upon which she was now proceeding to spread fresh sheets.

"Pedro and I sleep there," José explained easily. "But to-night we shall share it . . . you and me. Pedro will stretch upon the couch . . . won't you, old horse?"

"Without a doubt," said Pedro agreeably. "And with great comfort."

Nicholas took a sharp breath. He had never slept with anyone in his life and his skin contracted slightly at the prospect. But no one seemed to notice his hesitation. The five sisters, marshalled by their mother, said good night to him—each offering her hand and bobbing a formal little curtsy—then went with Maria to the other room. Pedro stood up and, glancing first at the weather, went out for five minutes to stretch his legs. José had taken up a tattered magazine with a shiny, coloured cover from the pile beside the wood box.

Uncertainly, Nicholas began to undress, dropping his clothes, one by one, on the nearest chair. An extraordinary timidity, a sense almost of shame, slowed all his actions. And one frightful difficulty oppressed his mind. But José, without looking up, spoke a few words; and, taking the utensil from beneath the bed, Nicholas turned his back. After that, it was much easier. Maria had laid out for him a long jacket of a queer shape, laundered to threadbare whiteness. He slipped it on, tied the long tapes that drew in the neck and waist, then jumped into bed where, pressed against the wall, he lay quite still.

Presently the old man returned, shuffled about the room, talked, as though to himself, in an undertone, fed a morsel of wood into the stove. Next came the creak of springs as the couch received him.

José sat just a little longer, rustling the pages at the table. When he got up he yawned, absently rubbed the back of his scalp, did a few bending exercises, removed his boots. Then, reaching to the mantel, he put out the light. A minute or two later he was beneath the sheets, lying beside Nicholas.

89

Something must have told him that his bedfellow was not asleep. He murmured:

"Are you all right, *amigo*? Plenty of room?"

"Yes," whispered Nicholas.

Gradually the little boy's body relaxed from its rigid position against the wall. The box-bed was feathery and snug. He fell softly into sleep.

TWELVE

ONE HOUR EARLIER, quite unaware of all that had taken place in his absence, Harrington Brande stepped from the east-bound train at Barcelona Central. Carrying his valise, he pushed through the clamorous ring of porters and passed rapidly along the archway which gave access to the Estacion Hotel. Here an indolent clerk assigned him to a room on the second floor overlooking the courtyard. It was not a good room but, contrary to his habit, he made no protest—at least, it afforded him the quiet which, above all things, he desired. In the crowded compartment all the way from Madrid he had been unable to focus his thoughts properly, but had sat there dull and heavy, his teeth grinding, his cheeks furrowed by a fixed and painful frown.

"Shall you want dinner, *señor*?"

Brande gazed, almost stupidly, at the man who had brought him up.

"No, nothing." Then he recollected he had not eaten since breakfast. "Yes . . . bring me something . . . anything . . . coffee and cold ham."

"Certainly, *señor*."

As the man turned to go the Consul stopped him.

"Wait. I wish you to take a telegram to the office."

From his desk he picked up a pad of forms and wrote out the message:

To Garcia, Villa Breza, San Jorge.

Meet me with car San Jorge station early train 7.45 a.m. to-morrow Tuesday.

Harrington Brande.

He tore off the form, handed it to the porter, spoke in a tone of authority:

"See that they send this at once. And leave word for them to call me at six o'clock in the morning."

The man inclined his head.

"Assuredly, *señor*."

When the door closed Brande began to pace up and down the room, his fists clenched, his eyebrows drawn together in a brooding line, demanding of himself, for the hundredth time, why he had been deceived by the wording of that official letter. It was a natural conclusion that he had drawn; he could not blame himself in any way. And yet . . . how blindly confident he had been. As he recollected how he had spoken to Burton, to little Nicholas, before his departure, how he had built a glittering structure upon hopes which proved purely illusory, a sweat of bitter anguish broke out all over his body.

By a tremendous effort, he controlled himself, recalled to reason by a sense of his own weariness and the sight of his haggard, unshaven face reflected in the wardrobe mirror. He opened the valise, took out some toilet articles and went into the bathroom. While he ran the bath, he shaved, then lay, for some time, in hot water as though trying to soak out a physical hurt.

Afterwards, in dressing-gown and slippers, he sat down at the tray which had been placed upon the writing-table by the door. Quickly, he gulped down two cups of coffee, ate a buttered roll and a slice of ham. His appetite was soon satisfied. He got to his feet again and rang for the waiter to clear away.

The man came and went. Then the Consul was alone again, alone with his thoughts, with the burning memory

91

of his humiliation. A nervous tic started in his cheek as he turned again to the writing-table, placed several sheets before him on the blotter, seized a pen, and began:

Estacion Hotel,
Barcelona.
Monday, 10.30 p.m.

Dear Halevy,—I write from this hotel, driven by the desire to unburden myself to you—my friend and physician—and by the urgent need for your counsel and support.

You are well aware of the injustices which have dogged my official career—indeed, you have often complimented me on the dignity and fortitude with which I have sustained them. From my letters of last month, you knew of my efforts to settle down and make the best of my recent transference to the Costa Brava. There, on Friday last, I received a communication from Leighton Bailey, advising me that George Tenney, First Consul in Madrid, had suffered a paralytic stroke, and requesting my presence in the capital at once.

I am not a vain man, Halevy, as you well know. I never jump to conclusions. And I can assure you that the wording of this letter made it quite apparent that I had been chosen to replace Tenney. I proceeded with all dispatch to Madrid.

On Saturday, when I arrived, to my astonishment, I found it impossible to see Bailey—he had gone to the country for the week-end. And on Monday, when he returned, he stunned me with the announcement that I had been summoned merely as a stopgap, that Herbert Meyer, now in Warsaw, was to succeed Tenney and that 'he would be obliged if I filled in' on the secretariat till Meyer arrived.

I need not tell you how bitter was this blow. Yet I did not take it without protest. I dwelt, with some heat, upon my past services, upon the excellence of my record. I pointed out that my promotion was overdue. I asked him flatly to reconsider.

For a moment, Halevy, he did not answer. Then he said: 'You have quite an opinion of yourself.'

This impertinence was too much for me. I drew myself up.

92

I declared formally that I had my own work at San Jorge, that I had there, in my invalid son, a family tie of the most exacting nature and that, if I were not to have Tenney's post, I must ask him to excuse me from remaining in Madrid.

When I concluded, there was a silence. I had expected an angry outburst, but to my surprise Bailey began to smile as though, unaccountably, his perverted sense of humour had got the better of him. Then he said:

'You're a queer bird, Brande. I've often heard about you. You're a byword in the service. But you have to be seen to be believed. I ought to report you, of course. But I won't. Go back to San Jorge. And for God's sake try to be a human being. Lose some of your smugness, your colossal egoism. Bring yourself a little up to date. It may not get you promotion. But at least it might get you a bit more out of life.'

What could one reply to such a tirade? I bowed coldly, turned and left the room. Without hesitation or delay, I departed by the eleven o'clock train. And now, here I am, my good friend, in such a turmoil of bitterness, desolation and just resentment, I must throw myself upon your bounty, your skill as a healer of minds.

At this point Brande broke off, with a sudden engorgement of the veins upon his forehead. Could he continue? For his own sake, whatever the pain to himself, he must. How often, in the past, relaxed upon the Professor's couch, in the narrow consulting-room off the Rue des Capucines, the sound of traffic muted by the thick, drawn curtains, he had found benefit in complete, uninhibited self-revelation and in submitting, with closed eyes, to the murmured injunctions of the skilled psychiatrist, seated in the obscurity behind him. Now, even at this distance, he felt the urgent need of some such solace. Setting his teeth, he resumed:

What I must tell you is this, Halevy, although I do so at the risk of losing my self-respect. When Bailey spoke these out-

93

rageous words to me a dizziness overcame me, and I had the strange, the horrible illusion that it was my wife who uttered them. In the mist which swam before me, I seemed to see her, in the rain, as she emerged that night, alone, from her lodging on Thirty-ninth Street in New York. I had followed her there, had waited outside, for at least two hours, convinced that she had been receiving the visit of a lover. When I stepped out of the shadow and confronted her, the lamplight shone full upon her pale face, upon her incredulous eyes, and she said . . . but, my God, there is no need for me to torture myself . . . you must remember that incident, for I revealed it to you in full—as though tearing it from my heart—the first time I submitted myself to you for analysis.

You see, my friend, how deeply this has upset me. No doubt there is scant importance in Bailey's insulting words; they are too absurd to be credible. But what of my reaction to them? Will these still bleeding wounds which you alone know of, and have probed so gently, never heal? Will my desire to be loved, to be loved tenderly, passionately, exclusively, never be fulfilled? Am I one of these figures, destined always to be misunderstood, misjudged, mistreated by lesser spirits? Will due recognition of mind and heart never be mine?

And what, dear friend, of the future?

I cannot deny that I value in some degree the status which attaches to the rank of Consul. Moreover, I consider that I am naturally fitted to carry out the official duties and functions thereby involved. Nevertheless, there is a point beyond which one cannot force the most willing heart, when one must draw up and in a solemn tone cry, 'Halt!'

You know that my work on Malbranche is now practically complete and will, I expect, be issued to the world within the next three months. Without presumption, one cannot but believe that this monumental creation, now almost a part of myself, will cause a stir in the intellectual and philosophical circles of both continents. If so, should I not resign from the service and devote myself exclusively to literature? I have some means of my own which would relieve me from a vulgar de-

pendence upon the public. And above all I have to consider the welfare and best interests of my dear son.

At a time like this, Halevy, when the human soul is sunk in deep despondency, one cannot but thank God for the blessing of Nicholas. From what I have revealed to you, under the seal of professional secrecy, you must realise how much the tragedy of my marriage has been compensated for by the sweet, pure, and overflowing love which my son bears for me. Were I a free agent—for one may ply one's pen in any latitude—might this not be reflected favourably upon my child's delicate health? We could visit those spas most likely to improve his nervous diathesis. (Indeed, my own highly-strung system would probably benefit thereby also.) I should be able to devote myself exclusively to him, to safeguard him from all adverse and evil influences in the difficult years of puberty . . . ah, yes, to watch over and protect the blooming of my tender flower.

You alone, my dear doctor, can advise me upon such a decision. Therefore I entreat you to advance your promised visit to the Casa Breza. You had arranged to visit us in June. Instead, come now, or at least within the next two weeks. You will be made royally welcome. It is not as though you were dependent upon the exigencies of ordinary practice. And one of your colleagues can take over at the clinic. Do not fail me.

It is nearly midnight. I must get some sleep . . . even if it means taking four of these tablets which you gave me and which now, alas! seem to be losing their effect. Surely I have written enough to convince you of my need. I repeat, do not fail me. I look forward within the next few days to your reply. Meantime, I shall take things quietly with Nicholas, lick my wounds, as it were, and renew myself in the sunshine of his smile.

Your devoted and suffering friend,

Harrington Brande.

With his head supported by spread-out fingers, the Consul sat motionless except for the imperceptible twitching of his facial nerve. A surging self-pity, that familiar, swelling sense of martyrdom, still suffused his breast. Yet he felt better for

95

having written the letter, purged of something of his distress. It was, in a minor degree, the same 'cleansed' feeling which came to him after these cathartic séances in the Professor's consulting-room. He sighed, and gradually his chin elevated itself in a gesture of renewed fortitude. Without haste, he rose, went out of the room and, at the lift shaft, posted the letter. An hour later, aided by the drug, he was sunk in the oblivion of sleep.

THIRTEEN

FOR ONCE THE coastal train was punctual. At fifteen minutes to eight next morning, Harrington Brande arrived in San Jorge, and on the platform found Garcia awaiting him.

"You received my telegram," he remarked, surrendering his valise and stepping towards the car.

"Yes, señor. But why did you not permit me to fetch you from Barcelona? To suit your convenience, I could have journeyed through the night."

Despite the bleakness of his mood, the Consul experienced a faint glow at the man's solicitude—this Garcia was indeed an exceptional fellow. Not often did he unbend to his servants, but as the butler tucked the rug round his knees he answered:

"You serve me well, Garcia . . . for that reason it pleases me to show you some consideration in return."

They drove off. The streets, damp with the morning dew, were quite deserted, and in five minutes they drew up at the front door of the villa. With a sense of homecoming, of tender expectancy, relieving the heavy oppression in his breast, Brande descended from the automobile. He had half hoped that Nicholas might be on the *patio* to greet him, but that, after all, would have been an infringement of the rules he had himself laid down for the boy. Gravely, yet hastening a little, he passed into the hall and went upstairs with Garcia behind him, carrying the bag. First he went to his own room, removed his travelling coat and washed his hands, then, with a deepening of his anticipation, passed through the communicating door to his son's apartment. But no sooner had he crossed the threshold than he drew up, his smile fading, his eyes puzzled and perplexed. Where was Nicholas? Could the boy be hiding, playing a childish trick upon him? No. The bed had not been slept in. The room was completely empty.

With an altered face the Consul swung round.

"Garcia! Garcia! Where is my son?"

The man put down the valise with a careful touch and, straightening himself, gazed with impassive features at a spot two inches above his master's head.

"Your son, señor? I regret to tell you that ... he is not here."

"What!"

"Yes, señor." The butler spoke softly, as though caressing the words which slid between his lips. "Yesterday afternoon ... before Magdalena and I could intervene ... he went away."

Harrington Brande stared at the other, his first stupefaction mounting rapidly to alarm.

"Where did he go? And with whom?"

"I do not know precisely where he went, señor ... to the town, I think." Garcia paused, his eyes flickering with little tongues of darkness as, in a tone that was almost inaudible, he added: "He went with José."

"José!" From between clenched teeth the Consul echoed that hateful name.

"None other, señor. They went laughing and talking ... arm in arm." Garcia paused, assumed a note of false reassurance. "Oh, have no fear, señor. They will return this morning. Assuredly. It was only last night they spent together."

The Consul felt his legs give way. Deathly pale, he sat down upon the edge of the bed. José with his son ... in spite of his express command ... and when he had believed their association ended. The phrases 'laughing and talking . . . arm in arm . . . they spent last night together . . .' seared like hot irons upon his brain. He clenched his hands as a hell-fire of rage, hatred, and frustrated love blazed up within his breast. God in Heaven, that this should happen to him, in his deepest hour of trial, when he had returned overflowing with paternal tenderness, with a greater need of filial affection than ever before! At the thought, a swift revulsion of feeling seized him. No, no, it was incredible . . . he could not . . . he would not believe it.

"Garcia," he exclaimed feverishly. "What you tell me is impossible. . . . My son must have gone to visit Mr. Burton. There is some mistake."

The butler, watching him intently with those darkly burning eyes, in a secret ecstasy of mockery, shrugged his shoulders slightly.

"It is not my place to contradict you, señor. Always it could be said of me that I know my place. And that place has often been a high one. Of course, if you suggest that I am departing from the truth . . ."

"No, Garcia." Brande's gaze sought out the other in a strange, dependent manner. "That is the last thing . . . you are above suspicion. But still . . ." He broke off, pressing both hands against his brow.

"It is very hard, no doubt, for the señor to believe." Free of the Consul's scrutiny, Garcia, beneath his impassive stillness, seemed to quiver with dæmonic mirth. "I have the utmost respect for the señor and his son. I hesitate to inflict pain upon the señor. Yet if it should come to a question of proof . . ."

As, with infinite effort, Harrington Brande raised his head, Garcia held out to him a creased sheet of paper.

"I found it, señor, crushed up, in the garden. There are others. But perhaps this is enough."

Mechanically, the Consul accepted the paper, but so blurred was his vision he could make nothing of the pencilled scrawl which covered it except the word 'love.' To gain time,

98

he fumbled for his glasses, then, with a heart like lead, he put them on.

'*Oh, dearest José, how I love to be with you, every minute of my time. . . .*'

He read the sheet through, in that strange automatic manner, read all the tender messages which had passed so playfully between José and his son. At first, a faint flush stained his temples, but it faded swiftly, leaving the drawn face paler, more frozen than before. He felt blank and dazed, with a hollow sickness in his stomach, but out of the vacancy there surged a stark and suffocating anger.

A low exclamation from Garcia penetrated through the rust-coloured haze which swirled about Harrington Brande.

"They have returned, *señor*." The butler pointed through the window. "Look, there . . . in the garden."

There was a pause. Without moving the Consul answered:

"Thank you, Garcia. That will be all for the present. I shall see my son at once."

He remained seated for some minutes after the man had gone, then stiffly, he got to his feet, filled his stifling lungs with a convulsive breath. Inexplicably, he could not bring himself to look through the window into the garden. He turned and went slowly downstairs. Then, as he reached the hall, the front door swung open and in a burst of sunshine Nicholas ran into the house.

He saw his father immediately, started perceptibly and, with a stifled cry, drew up short. All the brightness went out of his eyes. It made no difference that he came forward quickly with a smile of welcome, the Consul had observed upon his son's face that first flicker of fear, and again that surging vortex choked his heart.

"Good morning, Nicholas," he said in a dead voice.

"Good morning, Father," the boy faltered.

"Have you had breakfast?"

"Yes, Father."

99

"Ah! You are more fortunate than I. Perhaps, if you have nothing better to do, you will bear with me while I have mine."

He led the way into the dining-room, followed by Nicholas, and took his place at the table, on which Garcia presently placed the familiar tray of coffee, fruit and rolls. The Consul poured himself a cup of coffee with a hand which, incredibly, was steady. He had not asked his son to sit down, and the boy stood facing him like a prisoner at the bar. Having seen that everything was in order, Garcia noiselessly withdrew.

"When I arrived this morning," the Consul began, "I had hoped, possibly presumptuously, that you would be on hand to greet me."

"But, Father . . . I didn't know you were coming back so early."

"Obviously not." Brande's lips were twisted by a bitter spasm. "But that apart . . . where have you been?"

"With José."

"You spent last night at his house?"

"Yes, Father."

The Consul broke a roll.

"I understand that you had given me your word not to speak to him."

"I didn't, at the beginning, Father. Then I only spoke a little." Moisture was starting in the boy's eyes. "But in the end I had to. I felt so lonely . . . and so frightened."

"Indeed. Frightened of whom, might I ask?"

From beneath his long lashes, Nicholas stole a timid glance towards the pantry door. In an extremely low voice he answered.

"Of Garcia, Father."

"What?" The Consul sat up abruptly, with an air of outrage. "How can you tell me such a lie?"

"I'm not lying, Father. He did frighten me, only Magdalena asked me not to tell you why. That's the true reason I went home with José, Father. Oh, please believe me, please."

"I do not believe you," Brande answered sternly. "You

100

are deliberately making up this absurd story for the sole purpose of deceiving me."

"No, no, Father. I beg you to believe me." Tears, welling from behind his smarting eyeballs, trickled down Nicholas' nose and cheek. "If I must tell you . . . Garcia was frightful. He had the knife. He chopped the head off my little fish. The blood ran all over the table. I thought he was going to kill me too. Oh, can't you see it, Father? He's not what he pretends to be . . . he makes a mock of us all the time. He's bad and wicked, indeed he is, he's not a good man like you and José."

"How dare you couple me with him?" shouted the Consul, the blood rushing to his brow.

Nicholas stiffened, drew back from the livid face before him, then burst into a paroxysm of sobs.

"Are you out of your wits?" Brande went on hoarsely. "Drivelling about knives and blood and chopping heads off. Someone has put you up to this . . . to slander Garcia. I won't have it. Garcia is above reproach, a thoroughly reliable person, utterly superior to this . . . this gutter-lout of yours."

"No, no, Father." Nicholas wept. "José is nice."

The Consul ground his teeth in an access of fury so violent it swept through his head like the fumes of ether. He had to grip the arms of the chair to hold himself in check— clinging desperately, as it were, to his one point of vantage— the chill throne of the inquisitor.

"So your friend is nice." He seemed to gasp for breath. "You like him?"

"Yes, Father."

"You may even love him?"

The little boy nodded through his tears.

"Aren't we supposed to love everyone?"

The Consul drew back as though a viper had stung him.

"Don't prevaricate with me, sir. Tell me at once. Where did he take you last night?"

"To his home."

"Where is that?"

101

"In the Calle Corriente."

"I see. The worst slum in San Jorge."

"Oh, it isn't really, Father," Nicholas gulped. "It's terribly clean. It has a view of the mountains, and butterflies and humming-birds on the walls. José collected them ... mounted them too ... and made the cases all by himself. And we had *olla podrida*, the best stew I ever tasted. Paquita cooked it. ... Maria couldn't, because she works so hard at the wash-house ... and old Pedro doesn't do anything but knit. ..."

He faltered and broke off, stifled by the look upon his father's face. He did not understand that in his childish effort to explain, to propitiate, he had fanned the flames within the Consul's breast to an even whiter heat. He began to cry again, worse than ever.

"It is pleasing to your father to learn of the degree of intimacy which has been achieved between his son and this rabble." The voice tightened. "Go on, sir. What else took place?"

The child's breast, racked by sobs, took a great heave.

"We played *estallido*, father ... a game of cards. ..."

"Who played?"

"All of us."

"Whom do you mean by all of us?"

"José and Pedro ... and me ... with Paquita, Juana, Luisa, Elena, and Bianca. Oh, I'm sorry, Father. I forgot. Maria didn't play. She was putting fresh linen on the bed."

The erect figure in the chair grew suddenly more rigid.

"On whose bed?"

"José's and mine."

The Consul's brain reeled. In his emotion he leaned forward slightly as though proffering himself for a blow.

"You and he ..." He whispered huskily, then could say no more.

A silence followed, so absolute and sterile it froze even the child's rasping sobs. Involuntarily, Nicholas began to tremble. His appalled and tear-drenched vision seemed suddenly to magnify the apparition of his father, seated

102

there with stricken brow and cheeks the colour of tallow.

"What . . . oh, what have I done, Father?"

The Consul rose, plucking at the stiff, immaculate collar which encased his throat, took a few paces, almost lost his balance. Then, holding on to the mantelpiece, his head averted, he spoke in a strangled voice:

"Leave me. . . . Go upstairs to your room for the present. I shall see you later."

Another silence, more hollow, more sterile than the first. For many moments after his son had crept out of the room Brande remained bowed, in wild, chaotic thought, by the empty fireplace. At last a deep breath of decision whistled through his dry lips. Yes . . . that was the best, the only course. No matter how great a man's capabilities might be, there were certain situations in which he must perforce seek expert help.

Heavily, as though holding himself together, the Consul crossed the hall into the salon, seated himself at the escritoire in the embrasure, took up his pen and wrote.

To Professor Eugene Halevy, 219^b Rue des Capucines, Paris, France. Leave everything and come here immediately. The matter is vital and urgent.

Harrington Brande.

He rang the bell, and when Garcia appeared handed him the note.

"Take the car into town and send this telegram at once."

"Yes, *señor*."

Brande remained seated in the embrasure. The speedy purr of the automobile steadied him somewhat. Then his gaze, lifting unguardedly, passed through the window panes into the garden, and the flame sprang out in his heart again, nearly suffocating him.

The gardener stood on the edge of the bright lawn, naked to the waist, young thighs planted well apart, his golden-skinned torso gleaming in the sunlight, swinging the scythe

103

with easy strokes. Fascinated, scarcely breathing, Brande watched the splendid rhythm, every sweep cutting into his flesh. In a sweat of hatred, his fingers twitched and clenched upon the pen, snapping it off short. But he did not notice. Lost in a whirling lust, he still watched, with dilated pupils and throbbing eardrums, that clean, glittering blade, sweeping and sweeping in a perfect arc, sweeping like a scimitar, against the faraway blue mountains.

FOURTEEN

WITHIN FOUR HOURS a telegram from Paris was delivered at the Casa Breza:

Arriving to-morrow Thursday 5.30 p.m. Till then advise complete calm. Devotedly Halevy.

The Professor was as good as his word. Next day, when the afternoon train jolted into San Jorge Station, a little man, precise and almost priestly, of a pale complexion, with small but penetrating eyes set deep in a narrow head, and a trimmed wisp of imperial on his small chin, clad in a black travelling cape and crushed dark hat, descended nimbly from the coach and clasped Harrington Brande's stiff fingers between both his small, soft hands.

"My poor friend!" Absorbing, with one adroit glance, the Consul's dark and fretful gloom, his manner seemed to say: I am here now, I forbid all further worry.

The weather had turned cold, and as they entered the car and glided off a fine rain was falling, veiling the lines of the harbour, obscuring a grey and motionless sea.

"I had your letter." Halevy made the remark, gazing straight ahead. "But now . . . your situation has deteriorated?"

"It is infinitely worse," Brande broke out in a low and concentrated tone. He was about to proceed when Halevy,

104

with an authoritative pressure on his knee, primly restrained him.

"Not now, my friend. We have plenty of time. Relax. I am at your disposal for as long as may be necessary."

They reached the villa in this enforced silence and swept beneath the dripping mimosas, whose slender branches hung low, pendant with crystal drops. The cliffs were swathed in ghostly vapours, the mountains blanketed with cloud. The air, alive with whispers, held the sound of unseen rivulets, trickling and seeping into the dank yet insatiable earth, and from far off, through the sea fog, the melancholy wail of a fisherman's conch rose and fell, again, again, falling and fading, like a spent star, into the outer desolation.

But within the house much preparation had been made, fires blazed in the dining-room, the salon, and in the large guest bedroom, filling the air with warmth and the incense of fragrant cedarwood. In the kitchen Magdalena moved massively, and Garcia, with his swift, gliding step, was up and down the stairs a dozen times.

Dinner for two, served at eight o'clock, was near enough perfection to cause the Professor—who, despite his clerical air, clearly had no aversion to the good things of the table —to compliment the Consul upon his cook, and to chide him for failing to do justice to her art. At intervals, as he ate his crawfish *espagnol*, under the shaded candles, he directed towards his host that glance of hooded inquiry, fully cogniz-ant of the intensity of Brande's suffering, yet resolved to hurry nothing, to carry out, unruffled, his technique of delayed observation, to remain, as always, master of the situation.

Eugene Halevy, son of a Brest ship's chandler, had come to Paris, a raw and undergrown lad, some twenty years before, to study medicine and, after several failures in the preliminary examinations, he took an ordinary diploma. About that time the fame of Charcot had reached its height, and amongst the crowd attracted by that brightness was young Dr. Halevy. He attended the great man's lectures, haunted his wards in the Salpetrière and, being chosen—at random—to assist once or twice during the celebrated mass-hysteria demonstrations, decided he must specialise in psychiatry.

Beyond a certain provincial sharpness, which gave him an aptitude for picking up the phrases and mannerisms of his chief, Halevy had no qualifications for this type of work. But, aided by a modest inheritance from his father, he went to Vienna, studied under Jung, took a course at Heidelberg, spent eighteen months in the great mental asylum of Mecklenburg. When he returned to Paris he was admitted, on the strength of this experience, to the staff of the Institute Nervosthenique, a small clinic, situated in Passy. Also he began to deliver lectures of a semi-popular nature at the Academy of Mental Hygiene. Gradually he acquired a limited clientele, including the usual following of female neurotics, of borderline cases, and *malades imaginaires*. His manner, as might be expected, had improved, his eyes were keener, his hands more adroit, he affected a frock-coat and high black stock which gave him, a confirmed bachelor, the look of a clerical savant. Master of hocus-pocus, he flourished, day by day, on the anxieties and pitiful avowals fed into his ears. He learned to be cruel, to extort secrets with a single word, to utter paradoxes and predictions with a kind of sinister seriousness, strangely at odds with his meagre figure.

One summer, during a brief vacation at Knocke, his visit had come to the notice of Harrington Brande, who at that time was officially stationed in this Belgian resort. The Consul, afflicted by his periodic melancholia, had, on an impulse—the most fortunate of his life, he afterwards declared—taken the fateful decision to consult the Parisian psychiatrist. Immediately an affinity was manifest between these two mediocrities, so different in temperament, so similar in type. Many times thereafter Brande sought out his new physician, who alone seemed to bring him benefit. From the long séances in the Rue des Capucines a tenacious friendship grew between the dignified, frustrated official and

106

the little false priest who heard, scientifically, his closest secrets, and was, thereafter, in growing ascendancy, his master.

When dinner was over the two men went into the salon, seated themselves on either side of the marble hearth. The gaslight in the lustre chandelier was low, the long, decorous room made ruddy by leaping tongues of firelight flickering like troops of phantoms across the spurious tapestries, the ridiculous consoles, the serpentine tables of spindly gilt. Halevy, aware that the point had been reached beyond which his friend could not be restrained, made with his head a motion of assent, significant, almost magisterial. Sunk deep in the chair, he inclined his brow against his thin hand, half covering his eyes and, his head averted like an abbé within his confessional, set himself to listen.

Immediately, the Consul's tight lips parted and his testimony broke forth, unsparing from the beginning, full and pitiless. Without appearing to watch him, the Professor, from between his parted fingers, missed nothing of the other's emotion, and although his face revealed merely a professional blankness, his stealthy, deep-set eyes had the stabbing sharpness of a lancet. Yet when, in conclusion, Brande fumbled in the pocket of his frogged velvet smoking jacket and handed him the scribbled sheet of paper, the gleam in his gaze was masked immediately. While in a frenzy of unrest the Consul sat wiping his damp forehead, Halevy deliberately mounted his gold-rimmed pince-nez and methodically read the document twice. Then, his lips pursed, exposing his anaemic gums, he began to nod his head.

"My good friend," he said at last, in a grave tone, "I will not deny that I view this unfortunate affair in a serious light. Were I less attached to you, I might pretend to gloss it over. Had I a slighter regard for your intelligence, I should perhaps withhold from you certain of the darker implications involved. But you are my friend, a man of the highest faculties and, although a father, a sophisticated citizen of the world. You know that filth exists even in the most unsuspected

107

places. That the sweetest flowers are nourished by the dung-hill, that the fairest forest pool, on which pure lilies grow, conceals beneath the surface a bed of muddy ordure."

The Consul started, but before he could interrupt Halevy mercilessly went on:

"Innocence, my friend ... what is it? We psychiatrists can afford to smile at that preposterous word ... the sentimental trade-mark of an obsolete faith. Do we not every day un-cover fresh running sores, new evidence of human vileness? Are we not all the servants of our bodies, victims of the terrors and disgusts of our desires? Why, even the first involuntary acts of infants, their clinging and clasping, the sensual ferocity with which they seize the maternal breast ..." He broke off with a dispassionate shrug. "As for the period which your son is now approaching, ah, there, indeed, we are faced with darker forces, with strange obsessions and hidden longings. . . . It is indeed unfortunate that, under these circumstances, this imprudent association with an older youth, a Spaniard too, should have arisen."

The Consul groaned, his hands so tightly clenched that the nails cut into his palms.

"You do not believe that Nicholas has suffered serious harm?"

"I do indeed fear that damage has been done," Halevy answered impartially. "How much or how little it is my place to discover."

"To discover?"

"Certainly. Much as I deplore it, I shall be obliged to submit your son to an analysis."

Brande started back, in sudden misgiving, filled by a perturbation of his whole being.

"But, surely . . ." he protested, in a faltering tone. "The child is so young, so upset at this moment, his sensibilities so delicate. . . ."

Halevy fixed the Consul with a cold glance.

"Do you doubt my professional skill?"

108

"No, no . . . dear friend . . . only . . . but if you think it necessary."

"Imperative." The Professor flung out the word conclusively, with an acid, injured air. "How other than by probing the subconscious can we discover what took place during these dangerous nocturnal hours?"

"Stop . . . Halevy." The Consul clutched his brow, as though the top of his head were coming off.

"Come, come, my friend," said Halevy with a kind of patronising brutality. "We ourselves are no longer children."

"No," the other stammered, overwhelmed, lowering his eyes. "Nevertheless . . . you know the state of my own health . . . what I have already suffered through my disastrous marriage . . . the strains and stresses of my official position . . . the prolonged creative effort of my literary work . . . and above all this, the overpowering love which I bear towards my son. . . ."

"I assure you I shall be as compassionate as I can," Halevy interjected stiffly. "I am not without experience."

"I trust you implicitly, dear friend," Brande stuttered, driven by his anguish to a kind of frenzy. "It is the brazen, shameless audacity of this fellow which maddens me."

"You have not dismissed him?" Halevy inquired, quickly.

Blindly, the Consul shook his head.

"Good," said the Professor approvingly, from between pursed lips. "We shall certainly subject him to a fairly strenuous examination. It may also be necessary for me to interrogate your indoor servants. You have no objection?"

"None. They are an excellent couple. It is this other . . . this José."

As he, again, pronounced that name, the rage and hatred in his heart overcame him. Leaning forward, with bursting eyeballs, he brought his fist down on the frail arm of the chair with homicidal fury, and cried:

"He must be punished."

The Professor inclined his head, again sent out his stealthy glance, which searched like a tentacle, and then withdrew.

109

He paused for a moment, pressing his finger-tips together. Then a strange smile began to play in the folds of his yellow cheeks—the tired smile of one who knows the abject secrets of mankind and is the privileged witness of their disguises, the keeper of their souls.

"Without a doubt, my friend . . . you did well to send for me."

FIFTEEN

NEXT MORNING THE rain had ceased, the skies once again were halcyon, and the earth, refreshed, basked in the radiance of a brilliant sun. To Nicholas, gazing wistfully into the garden from his bedroom window—which, greatly daring, he had opened a little way—the balmy air, sweet with fragile perfumes distilled by the alchemy of dawn, seemed to hold the promise of better things. Perhaps to-day he might be released from his cheerless confinement to his room. Now that Professor Halevy had come upon a visit—he had listened last night, with subdued interest, to the sounds of the guest's arrival—surely his father's mood would soften. The Consul was always at his best in the society of his Paris doctor.

Meanwhile, Nicholas had made an indifferent breakfast from his usual tray and, dressed in shirt and trousers, was watching intently for the signal that José would make from behind the tool-shed, the swift, outward wave of the arm, directed towards the upper window which, during these two days of enforced separation, had been the sole means of communication between them. Yet only to see that vigorous, reassuring gesture, so charged with meaning and affection, was enough to bring a healing comfort to the little boy's heart. He knew then that José had not forgotten him, That was enough. Whatever happened to him, more attacks of illness, the dreadful fulfilment of Garcia's threats, even the

110

visitation of his father's anger—nothing mattered if José remained his loyal, his loving friend.

It was now almost ten o'clock. José, raking the rain-channelled drive, had begun to move slowly in the direction of the shed where he would be screened from the lower windows of the house. Nicholas's pulse was already quickening in anticipation when he heard footsteps in the passage outside, and almost at once the door opened to admit his father and Professor Halevy. He spun round, defensively, his startled blush making him look guilty.

"Good morning, my child." Halevy nodded amiably.

"Good morning, sir," Nicholas answered. "Good morning, Father."

A pause followed which the boy, glancing sharply from one to the other, felt as oddly ominous.

The Consul cleared his throat, spoke in a constrained voice.

"Nicholas, since we are so fortunate as to have Professor Halevy with us, I have asked him to look you over and to reassure me of the state of your health." He glanced at Halevy. "You do not wish me to remain, I imagine."

"We shall manage excellently ourselves, my dear fellow," responded the Professor briskly, and as Brande, sombrely inclining his head, passed from the room, he turned to Nicholas with that same sly air of collusion. "There are some things we don't want even Father to know. Eh, my boy? Now, if you will just stretch out on your bed, we shall get along without the slightest trouble."

Nicholas stared back at the Professor with surprised perplexity. Accustomed though he was to the medical ritual periodically performed upon his frail body—Halevy had in fact 'looked him over' on several previous occasions—the boy sensed nevertheless in this particular approach, in the strange archness of the physician's manner, a new and more disturbing method. And when he had obediently lain down it was at once apparent to him that the Professor's examination, his manipulation of the stethoscope, all his tappings

111

and soundings, accompanied by reassuring murmurs and little precise movements of his hands, were no more than cursory, a performance cleverly designed to allay suspicion. And indeed, this misgiving was confirmed when a few minutes later Halevy rose and closed both the shutters, exclaiming:

"That sunlight is most trying to the eyes. There! Isn't that much more comfortable?"

In the dimness which ensued he slipped back, seated himself at the head of the bed, and placed his hand lightly on the little boy's forehead.

"We've known each other a long time, Nicholas." He spoke quite gaily. "I'm sure you look upon me as a friend, rather than a physician. You're not at all afraid of me?"

Since an answer seemed to be expected of him, Nicholas, lying on his back with his eyes on the ceiling, mumbled:

"No."

"Good," rejoined the Professor, in a more tempered tone. "I want you to feel, above all, that you can talk to me freely, just as you would to another boy. . . . Incidentally"—above the grey imperial the psychiatrist's yellow teeth bared in that same confederate's smile—"you are growing into a big boy yourself . . . which must make quite a difference to your ideas . . . your thoughts about life. It's these thoughts I'd like to hear about . . . and you needn't hesitate to tell me anything, the most shocking thing in the world. Now what, for example, are you thinking about now?"

"I don't know," Nicholas answered after a moment.

"Oh, come, my dear chap," jested the Professor, but softly. "Nature abhors a vacuum. I'm sure that clever little head of yours is not completely empty. Tee! hee! In fact, it's a Pandora's box, out of which you and I are going to bring the most remarkable things. Just imagine you are lifting the lid of that box. What is it you see at this moment? What is it that you feel?"

"I feel your fingers on my brow. They're like cotton-wool," Nicholas replied slowly, rather awkwardly. "And I see the

112

bars of light on the ceiling. They come from the shutters."

"Excellent," complimented the Professor. "Go on."

"About what?"

"Anything you wish . . . tell me the train of your thoughts . . . after the shutters. . . ."

"Well, I don't know," Nicholas said doubtfully. "They sort of give me the impression as if I were in a prison. It's so dark, you see, and these bars slanting all over the place rather make me want to get out."

"And if you were out, what would you do?"

"Go fishing," replied Nicholas without the slightest hesitation.

"Fishing?" echoed the psychiatrist, in the tone of one whom nothing amazed.

"Yes; that is what I'd do. I'd get on that lovely old creaky bus and drive right up into the mountains." Under the stroking fingers, a dreamy smile passed over the little boy's thin, upturned face. "Then I'd go down to the green valley and sit in the sun on the mill dam. I'd look at the cowslips and the wild irises, and the cork oaks. I'd bait my line and fish there in the pool all day long. And maybe I might catch an even bigger trout."

"You'd go alone, of course?" murmured the Professor, attentively.

"Of course not." The boy's remote smile deepened; he spoke without embarrassment. "José would come with me. He's the one who showed me how to do it."

"To do what?" breathed Halevy quickly.

"To fish, naturally. He's a wonderful fisherman. And the best *pelota* player in San Jorge. Yet he's so humble about it. And he works so hard, so awfully hard in the garden. . . ."

"You are fond of José?" prompted the Professor with inexhaustible suavity.

"Oh, yes, indeed I am . . ." cried the little boy. "José is my friend."

There was a brief silence in which the moted bars seemed to quiver with a strange pure light. The clairvoyant fingers maintained their measured rhythm, the murmurous voice resumed:

"When your father was away, you went to this river with José. And when the fishing was over, what did you do?"

"I had my *siesta*."

"With José?"

"Oh, yes, José lay beside me on the grass. It was so nice there, so warm in the sun."

"Of course," agreed this devil's confessor with a secret grimace. "I understand. I am not shocked, my child. Do not be frightened by what you tell me."

"But why should I be frightened?" Nicholas answered immediately. "I've done nothing wrong. I am only telling you the truth."

The Professor bit his lip and exclaimed, with momentary irritation:

"Surely you did wrong to disobey your father."

"I did not really mean to disobey him. It was chiefly because of Garcia."

"Ah!" said Halevy. "We will return to that in a moment. But meanwhile . . . you admit you are fond of José."

"I cannot help my feelings," Nicholas said seriously.

"No one is blaming you, my child." The psychiatrist's manner altered, became soothing again, as though once more he felt himself on safe and familiar ground. "I know you like José to be near you, to touch you. You would, for instance, rather it was he beside you now, stroking your hair . . ."

"Oh, much rather . . ." Nicholas exclaimed, and blushed suddenly for his unwitting rudeness.

But the Professor, delighted by that sign of shame, took no offence. The routine of his work had long made him indifferent to the worst insults, the most infamous abuse which distorted minds could heap upon him. He sought only to turn this childish confusion to his own advantage.

"And because you wished him to be near you . . . to touch

114

you"—he smiled confidingly—"that is why you went home with him?"

Nicholas moved uncomfortably, as though wishing he might look his hidden questioner in the face. This great dim room, the golden slatted beams which danced above him, the soft, persistent massage of his temples, all conspired to produce in him a pressing sense of lassitude in which complete acquiescence to these puzzling questions seemed the easiest, indeed the only course. Yet something within himself, the inner core of his fragile, childish spirit, forced him to resist.

"I do like José very much. . . ."

"You mean you love him," insinuated the Professor with a kind of holy gentleness.

"Well, yes, I love him." Nicholas' flush deepened. "But it was because of Garcia that I went home with him."

Halevy laughed shortly—how well he knew the value of that brief show of derision which, like an unexpected dagger thrust, had so often rent those veils of simulation which all his sympathy had failed to pierce.

"Garcia . . . always Garcia!" he threw out contemptuously. "I don't believe a word of it."

"It does not matter whether you believe me or not," Nicholas answered in a clear, proud voice, "so long as it is true."

There was another silence, sudden, arresting; and a slow wave of animosity crept under the Professor's impervious skin. This childish resistance, so unlooked-for, was exasperating in the extreme to a man of his experience. Not for an instant did he believe that Nicholas spoke the truth. In his universe, the world wherein he moved and breathed, normality had no place. Life was a steamy jungle, where unseen forces coiled and writhed in black and bitter mud. Well . . . he had dealt with delinquent children before, and cracked their armour in the end. He could entrap this stubbornness with a dozen tricks, each one of greater subtlety.

His poise regained, he smiled winningly at Nicholas and,

with an intensification of his ministering, his sacerdotal air, took possession of his arm.

"My dear child . . . I am grieved that you should so misunderstand me. I am not thinking in terms of right and wrong. So why should you defend yourself? I am on your side. What is called wickedness is no more than instinct, the legacy of a million years of primeval existence. Perhaps these big words confuse you, and that's the last thing we want. You must simply realise that angels no longer exist, that what you have done is only human. The danger lies in hiding it. If only you will lay it bare before me, then it becomes nothing . . . we can laugh at it together."

"Laugh at what?" asked Nicholas from between his teeth.

"This, for instance," murmured Halevy, casually producing the sheet of messages and holding it before the little boy's gaze.

Nicholas stiffened all over, as though braving himself against a blow; then his body gradually grew limp and he turned his clouded eyes away.

"Oh, it's nothing," murmured the Professor quickly, with a pacifying gesture. "But when you wrote like this, why pretend? You must have said much nicer things to José when you were alone with him . . . when you went to his home, for instance . . . and you were together during the night."

"We didn't say anything." Nicholas spoke dully, with averted head.

"But, my dear child," whispered this satanic prelate, bringing his cheek close to the boy's pillow, "you were there . . . just the two of you together . . . in the darkness. . . ."

A shiver passed over the child as though vaguely he were conscious of some unknown yet monstrous evil looming out of the shadows, pressing down upon him with irresistible insistence, striking fear and repulsion into his heart. Into what shameful kingdom of darkness and disgust was he being led? He wanted to throw himself from the bed, to run from the room, to disappear. Yet an overwhelming fatigue held him there, made him want to yield, to sue for mercy.

116

After all, what difference did it make? Why should he not accept this hidden meaning, eat of the poisoned fruit with which this man now enticed him? But at that moment an imperious order rose from the very depth of his being. He clenched his hands involuntarily and, with a great effort, wrenched himself free from the other's clasp, sat up defiantly on the bed. His face was very pale, his heart beating like mad. But he looked the Professor in the face, with all his strength, as though he were defending his life.

"I don't know what you want me to say. But I am not going to say it. I've told you I only went with José because Garcia scared me so badly. You can ask Magdalena, if you like. She will tell you. I wanted my father to ask her before."

The Professor concealed his mortification in a cold smile. He got to his feet, as though accepting a challenge he had long expected.

"Very well. We shall ask Magdalena."

Seated upright, his breath coming fast, Nicholas saw the Professor pull the tasselled cord twice, heard the faint jangling of the bell in the far-off recesses of the house. After a few minutes of straining silence, the heavy, sluggish footsteps of the cook sounded on the service stairs. A knock on the door. She entered.

"Magdalena," said the Professor, "it has been suggested that during the recent absence of your master, certain irregularities occurred in the household. In the first place, did Garcia remain in Barcelona on the night of Saturday?"

The woman, planted heavily by the doorway, stared stolidly at the Professor from beneath her brows. Her hands, slightly smeared with flour, hung away from her black dress.

"No," she said. "All the time, Garcia was here."

An electric shock passed through Nicholas. His body came forward with a jerk. Stupefied, his mouth trembling so that he could scarcely pronounce the words, he entreated:

"But, Magdalena . . ."

"Silence, please." Halevy returned his gaze to the cook.

117

"In the second place, did Garcia indulge in a drunken orgy on Sunday night?"

"No, señor . . ." Her motionless features might have been hewn out of wood. "Garcia does not drink."

"So he did not strike you, or frighten Nicholas in any way?" She shook her head.

"Garcia is a good man. It is well known. He never struck me in his life."

"Oh, Magdalena," Nicholas burst out in a heartbreaking tone, "how can you? You know he hit you. In the pantry. You were crying like anything. It was horrible. And he had the knife . . ." He broke off, overcome by a panic which seemed to rise sickeningly from his stomach.

"That will be all, Magdalena," Halevy said. "Thank you for bearing with us."

The cook stood a moment, as though scarcely aware that she was dismissed. Throughout the interview her bovine eyes had remained fixed dully, immovably, upon the Professor, but now, for an instant, they flickered towards Nicholas. She did not lose countenance; the downward curve of her lips remained unaltered, yet, with unexpected abruptness, she swung round and shuffled out.

With a cry of childish anguish, Nicholas collapsed on to the pillow, overwhelmed by this betrayal, tears pouring down his cheeks.

"Oh, José . . ." he whispered brokenly to himself. "Where are you, José? . . . What do they mean to do to us?"

Professor Halevy, his expression indecipherable, took one step forward, then halted. Several times he caressed his tufted chin, his narrow head cocked to one side, like a ferret ready to attack. No, he thought finally, not a word more. A little solitude, a few more tears, and the last resistance will vanish. Quietly, he reassured himself that the shutters were still tightly drawn, then, amidst that sound of muffled sobbing, he tiptoed from the room.

SIXTEEN

HARRINGTON BRANDE PAID only a cursory visit to the Consulate that morning, remaining there in a state of mounting tension for about an hour, before hastening back, with nerves a-quiver, to have luncheon with his house guest. Now the mournful meal was over, the Professor had made his report, and the two men sat in the dining-room, where coffee had been served to them.

"Then there is no doubt remaining in your mind." The Consul, with haggard face and bitter mouth, stirring his cup broodingly, at last broke the silence which had fallen upon them.

"None whatever." The Professor swallowed his coffee with every appearance of satisfaction. "That transference of the guilt complex is quite typical . . . and his breakdown, when he was confronted with Magdalena."

Brande's pale brow drew together in a sudden spasm.

"I hope it was not too severe a trial for my son."

"My dear friend . . . what are a few childish tears, a temporary heartache, against the major issue at stake?"

"He is not suffering now?" Again Brande groped for some alleviation of that anxiety which permeated the very marrow of his bones.

"Probably he is sound asleep . . . that is the usual sequel to a successful catharsis. In any case, you must not go near him. Solitude . . . opportunity for reflection . . . these are essential components of my treatment. I repeat—at all costs, these abnormal tendencies, which already seem tenacious, must be torn out by the roots."

Beneath the table, the Consul compressed his napkin into a hard, tight ball. Not looking at Halevy, he said:

"And José?"

The Professor put down his cup with a reflective frown.

"I cross-examined him at length this morning. A plausible

119

rascal." He hesitated. "I know how you feel about him, my dear Brande, but actually what can we do? You cannot take proceedings against him without inflicting enormous damage on Nicholas and yourself. The publicity alone . . . it's unthinkable."

"Something must be done." In a tone of menace, Brande bit out the words, his head sunk deep in his shoulders.

"Then be patient. If you give a fellow of that type enough rope, he's sure to hang himself. Why, Garcia let out, quite by accident, when I talked with him before lunch, that lately he's missed several small sums of money from his room. He didn't say it in so many words—he's too discreet for that—but I was sharp enough to see that he suspects José is the thief."

"What?" The Consul, absorbed in bitter brooding, spoke the word dully. Then gradually Halevy's meaning seemed to penetrate. He drew himself erect, his injected eye lit by a slow gleam. "Money stolen from Garcia . . ." he repeated. "This must be seen to without delay."

Before Halevy could answer, he reached out and rang the small silver bell which stood before him on the table. A longish pause followed. Then the butler appeared, buttoning on his white mess jacket, swallowing a last morsel of food.

"Forgive me, señor," he murmured. "I thought you had finished. Magdalena and I . . ."

"Yes, Garcia. I quite understand," broke in the Consul. "And I am sorry to disturb you at your meal. But a matter of extreme importance has just been brought to my notice. Is it the case that you have recently lost certain sums of money?"

"Lost, señor?" Garcia permitted himself the liberty of a slight shrug. "One does not lose money from a locked drawer in one's room."

"Ah! Then the money was stolen."

"Undoubtedly, señor. The lock was skilfully picked."

The Consul drew a deep, quick breath, as though he scarcely dared to hope.

"You take it very calmly, my good man."

120

Again Garcia shrugged, in a quiet yet disdainful manner.

"It was not a fortune, *señor*. Altogether, perhaps thirty or forty pesos were stolen. My philosophy of life does not permit me to regard that as a great disaster. Moreover, I have lived in great houses, like that of the de Aostas where I was forced to associate with dishonest colleagues. Nevertheless . . ." He paused, his eyes, inscrutable in that impassive mask, bent unblinkingly upon the Consul's face. "Nevertheless, *señor*, I am not calm."

"Why not?"

"Because, *señor*," Garcia answered, deliberately keeping those pale yet clouded eyes full upon the other, "I fear that some things of greater value have been stolen."

There was a dead silence. Brande's mouth had fallen agape. Halevy leaned across the table with every sign of interest.

"Yes," the butler resumed, shifting his gaze courteously to include the Professor. "I do not care to speak first; it is not my place. Nor do I desire to make trouble for another. But since you, yourself, raise the subject, I simply ask you, *señor* . . . what has become of those articles of value which you keep in the little box upon your dressing-table?"

The Consul licked his lips. His voice came queerly:

"You mean my evening studs—my cuff-links . . . ?"

"And your small flat watch with diamonds . . . the sapphire dress buttons . . . the signet ring . . . all your choice possessions." Garcia took up the enumeration gravely. "I observe them when I am valeting you, *señor*. And I have never seen finer."

It was true enough. The Consul from his private means had amply indulged a definite fondness for elegant *bijouterie* which, worn with full dress at official functions, set off his classic features and imposing figure to advantage, invested him with an appearance of superior rank.

With sudden decision he rose to his feet.

"Come with me, both of you."

He led the others upstairs, entered his bedroom. The round

121

morocco leather box stood in the centre of the dressing-table, flanked by yellowing ivory brushes and the heavy crystal flasks which held the Consul's bay rum and cologne. Without hesitation, Brande threw back the lid. The box was empty.

"My God!" he gasped. Seldom, if ever, was the Consul guilty of that exclamation, but now his whole body shook with an emotion so sudden and unearthly it could not otherwise be expressed.

"Rather careless of you, surely, not to lock it," Halevy murmured behind him.

Brande spun round with a congested face.

"I trust my people. Never before, in my experience.... All my jewellery. The intrinsic ... the sentimental value ... irreplaceable. ... Garcia, my good fellow, who has done this?"

The butler's lip curled slightly. He did not answer, but his gaze, travelling imperceptibly beyond the Consul, directed itself through the open window, and came to rest upon the garden.

"Yes," cried Brande with a strange lifting of his voice, a note almost of exaltation. "Remain here, Garcia. Will you come with me, Halevy? I should be glad of your support."

Accompanied by his friend, the Consul quitted the house and strode down the gravel path towards the tool-shed. José was not there. Checked, Brande was about to swing out towards the shrubbery, when his inflamed eye was arrested by the gardener's jacket drooping, shapelessly, from the rusted nail behind the door. A stifled exclamation broke from the Consul's lips. Always he prided himself upon his punctilious sense of honour. But now, borne forward by this fever of anger and resentment, he stepped without hesitation to the door and began to search the pockets of the coat, throwing recklessly upon the earth floor the useless objects which came to light—a ball of twine, some fish hooks stuck into a piece of cork, the dry heel of a loaf wrapped in newspaper, a lump of beeswax, an old horn spoon. There were many pockets in the patched and weather-stained garment

122

and a double lining as well, where perhaps a lad trained in country ways might hide and carry home a snared rabbit or a hare. Yet it seemed as though the exploration must prove fruitless when, suddenly, with a hoarse cry of triumph, the Consul brought out, yellow and glittering, from the innermost recess, a pair of heavy cuff-links.

"Mine!" he stuttered. "Unquestionably mine. And don't you see"—in his excitement he clutched Halevy's arm— "these are only gilt . . . the only imitation set I possess. He's got rid of all the rest . . . but these . . . because they have no real value . . . were left on his hands."

The Professor, with an air of justification, tilted his narrow head and murmured:

"Did I not tell you . . . only, my dear friend . . . for your own sake . . . for the sake of your health . . . be calm."

"I refuse to be calm!" Brande exclaimed in a kind of apocalyptic frenzy. "After all I have endured from him, the damage he has inflicted upon me and mine, at last he has been delivered up to me." He raised his voice and shouted: "José! Come here . . . immediately."

He had gathered himself to shout again when the sound of running footsteps became audible, and an instant later José broke into the little shed, pulled off his linen cap, and, between his quick breaths, exclaimed:

"You wanted me, *señor*."

"I do want you," Brande said thickly, in a voice which seemed choked with hate. He exposed the gilt cuff-links in his quivering palm. "Where did you get these?"

José looked at the yellow discs, bound by tiny chains, then his dark eyes passed from Halevy to the Consul.

"I do not understand you, *señor*. I have never seen these things before."

"Then explain how they got into your jacket."

"Impossible, *señor*." José's bewildered gaze darted towards the draggled *poncho* on the back of the door as though it too were the victim of some supernatural spite. "They were never there."

123

"They were there." The power which he now possessed of throwing back José's own words sent the blood mounting higher in the Consul's head. "I found them in your pocket a moment ago."

"No, señor." By contrast with Brande's overtones, the words came halting and confused.

"Professor Halevy can swear to it."

A bar of silence throbbed within the hut. José had turned quite white, his stare, as though fascinated, could not leave the glittering links.

"Someone must have put them there," he muttered at last.

A faint ironic snicker, instantly suppressed, escaped from the Professor's indrawn lips.

"The classic answer," he murmured to his friend.

But the Consul did not hear. The singing in his ears grew louder. He felt, again, that hot flame within his chest. He said, slowly, as savouring each word:

"I am going to summon the *guardia*. Meantime, you will come with us to the house. It is useless for you to try to escape."

A pause. José was paler than ever, deeply serious, with a strange distress in his pained eyes. Yet his lip drew back with a kind of trembling pride.

"I shall not run away, *señor*. The *guardia* is my friend. He knows I am not a thief."

The procession started towards the house, the Consul first, then José, Halevy bringing up the rear. Within, José was shut up in the dining-room and Brande himself telephoned the San Jorge Police barracks. They had not long to wait. Less than half an hour later a sergeant of the civil *guardia*, young and well-set-up in his dark green uniform and black, shiny hat, arrived at the front door. Garcia showed him to the Consul, who was at once impressed by the man's smart and soldierly appearance.

"I regret troubling you, sergeant," he began directly, "but it appears I have a thief in my employ."

Succinctly—for he had now fully recovered his self-

124

possession—he outlined the facts, a damning case. It seemed that when José's name was mentioned the *guardia* lost for a moment his look of calm alertness. And when Brande concluded he stood, studying his boots, in puzzled indecision.

"It sounds extremely bad, *señor*," he said at length. "Yet are you sure there is no mistake. I know this José Santero. He is perhaps a trifle wild . . . but a thief . . . ?"

The Consul drew himself up, his expression turning stern and official.

"Do you propose to allow your personal feelings to interfere with your duty?"

"No, no, *señor*," the sergeant answered hastily. "Let us see him at once."

They went into the dining-room, where José stood alone, in fixed and pained perplexity, awaiting them.

SEVENTEEN

FOR NICHOLAS IT was like sunshine after rain, to be allowed to dress and come downstairs, to have breakfast in the dining-room with his father and Professor Halevy, to be spared that utter solitude where, with the chilly tray rim pressed against his chest, he chewed without taste, his ears continually on the alert for new and formidable occurrences below. And although he was conscious of something hidden, a sense of conspiracy between them, that disturbing tension of the past few days seemed eased, as by some peculiar and unexpected intermission, and they were pleasant to him, in a distant sort of way. The Professor, nibbling at buttered toast, spoke down to him a good deal, in a smiling, noncommittal fashion, as though the inquisition of the day before had never occurred. His father, from behind the pages of the *Echo de Paris*, bent one or two covert glances towards him which, although still aloof, held a hint of reconciliation. And when the meal was over, and Nicholas sat very straight,

125

waiting for his orders, the Consul actually declared, with only a pretence of stiffness:

"You may wish to go into the garden this morning . . . you have been rather confined lately." He turned to Halevy in that same measured, rather studied manner. "I shall not go to the office until noon. If it does not altogether bore you, perhaps you might run through the final section of my manuscript."

"Delighted, my friend," Halevy replied, patting his lips delicately with his napkin.

They stood up. Nervous thrills were running all over Nicholas—these sessions upstairs had left him strangely shaken, and his legs, especially, did not perform too steadily. But with an effort he subdued his agitation, moved quietly to the front door and the next minute was standing on the portico.

Oh, how good it was to be outside again, to be free after the miseries of his detention—he sniffed the fresh, scented breeze with expanding nostrils. It would never do, of course, to rush at once towards José. With his hands by his sides, he strolled, very slowly and inconspicuously, down the herbaceous border, pausing every few steps to bend forward and smell the flowers. One of the pink curly rolls which edged the path had been displaced—carefully he put it back. Then he stood to study a snail as, with horns extended, it bore forward the domed burden of its castle, leaving behind a silvered trail. Out of the corner of his eye he saw Professor Halevy emerge from the villa, carrying a plaid rug and the precious bundle of the Malbranche manuscript. When the psychologist had settled himself comfortably in a long chair by the arbour, Nicholas edged off towards the cobbled stableyard, whither, for some time now, the sound of woodchopping had enticed him.

But it was Garcia who, with rolled-up sleeves, wielded the whirling machete, and in a flurry of disappointment and alarm the boy scurried round the gable of the coach-house towards the new rockery. The rockery looked well; the

126

hart's-tongue ferns were already spreading their tender green fronds over the mica-scaled stones. Yet José was not here. Hastening his steps, Nicholas passed beyond the oleanders, through the old myrtle patch, then back by the empty tool-shed and the catalpa tree until, finally, having completed the tour, he drew up, disconsolately, beside the arbour.

The Professor, comfortably enwrapped, balancing the heavy pile of sheets neatly clasped by metal strips, seemed too engrossed to be disturbed. But after some hesitation Nicholas ventured to approach. Halevy looked up, over the rim of his pince-nez.

"Excuse me, sir . . . have you seen the large watering-can?"

"No," said the Professor agreeably. "Have you?"

"I haven't," Nicholas answered. "And all the petunias want watering, very badly."

"Do they? . . . then perhaps you will find it."

"I don't know where it has been put . . . and even if I did, it's too heavy for me to lift."

"Then you had better dismiss it from your mind."

"But the petunias . . . someone should attend to them."

"I dare say they will survive."

There was a pause. Nicholas gazed about him dismally. The Professor's eyes were now fixed upon the priceless manuscript. Without raising his head, he replied:

"Dear child, I suggest you continue your stroll. I propose to have a conversation with you this evening. Meantime, I should be glad not to be disturbed."

Dashed, the little boy moved off. As the hatchet strokes still rang out he decided he might reach the back premises unobserved. Despite her unbelievable behaviour on the day before, which in any case seemed unreal and remote, he believed that Magdalena was still, more or less, his friend.

Yes, there she was, seated on the step of the open kitchen door, plucking the feathers from a chicken that lay across her knees. In the dark interior of the kitchen copper pans glinted on the shelves and a bunch of rosemary twigs crackled

127

on the hearth. With his hands in his pockets, he stood watching her through the little snowstorm which enveloped her. From her abrupt, violent movements, he knew she was in a bad humour, yet after a moment, in a low, coaxing voice, he said:

"Magdalena . . . where is José?"

She gave her head an angry shake and slapped the limp fowl over on its back so that its breast showed blue and tense.

"Go away. I don't know anything. I do not wish to know anything. I only work hard morning, noon, and night . . . work hard like a slave." Her voice rose suddenly to a high note and almost broke. "Do you hear me? Go away."

Nicholas went away. He went through the faded mimosa hedge, his feet pressing into the carpet of spent blossoms which lay beneath the bushes, and came out at the cliff wall. Here, on a flat stone, he seated himself and, with drooping lip, stared out at the empty bay. It was nothing, he told himself . . . perfectly all right . . . José would turn up in the afternoon, probably he had been sent somewhere on an errand.

A whiff of cigarette smoke made him turn his head, then, with a start, he almost toppled over. Garcia had come down from the stable yard, noiseless in his rope-soled sandals, and was now standing beside him, a burning stub between yellow fingers, sharing his admiration of the view.

"The sea," he remarked. "Is it not superb? Lying there, like a great beast, licking its paws?"

Nicholas, after an involuntary shiver, sat, contracted, on the stone. Yet he perceived that Garcia was in a mood of unusual contentment, suffused, it seemed, by some strange, unnatural felicity. The man's long slanting eyes were drowsy and his pin-point pupils sparkled with a sort of inner pleasure as he inhaled deeply from the cigarette.

"It is good to get away from people . . . mediocre, ridiculous people . . . and be at one with the eternal. I know the sea. I have sailed the oceans of the world. I have been becalmed in the blazing Sargasso. Weeds, weeds . . . green weeds

128

clinging under the surface scum, clinging like the tentacles of octopi." He threw away the spent cigarette and, pulling from his hip pocket a *librillo* of papers and a canvas bag, he tugged at the string with his sharp teeth, and began, with one hand, to roll himself another.

"I thought you were a soldier." Nicholas broke the silence in a quavering tone.

"Bah! I have been everything. A sailor too. Shanghaied. Two years before the mast. You do not believe me?" He slipped an arm from his open shirt and with a vehement gesture exposed his back, the smooth bare skin all seamed with whitish scars. "Now you can see where I was flogged ... flogged till the blood ran like a red river. Is that a crime? They could not make me yield. Never. When they brought bread and water, I sat like a king on his throne, in my cell."

"Cell?" gasped Nicholas, sitting there like a little scared bird, yet fascinated, too. "Were you in prison?"

Garcia, suddenly motionless, stared at Nicholas in a hard kind of way. The match he had just struck burned down to his fingers, yet he did not seem to feel it.

"Do not meddle with my affairs," he threatened. Then, lighting the cigarette, he burst into a fit of laughter. "Prison ... do you think it would be nice in prison?"

"No ..." stammered Nicholas.

"No?" Garcia laughed. "My God, you have said something true at last. Do you know the Spanish prisons, where the damp trickles down the walls and the cockroaches, big as rats, run over you at night? Where the stinking darkness is enough to shrivel up your heart? And the wall, the high wall, where men stand with rifles, seems to separate you even from the sky. Don't let yourself be trapped in there, little master. Be smart, like me, and stay outside."

"I will. I will," Nicholas fervently agreed. "No one would want to go to such a place."

"Ho, ho!" Garcia threw back his head in greater merriment. "You are more amusing than ever, little master. Of

TSG—9   129

course no one wants to go. But sometimes one is made to go. The *guardia* comes, clicks on the handcuffs, and drags one away." He paused, and added softly: "Like he did yesterday."

"Yesterday?" echoed Nicholas in a puzzled voice.

"You did not know?" Garcia, no longer laughing, fixed upon the boy his ironic and inhuman gaze, his pupils shrunk to nothing, quite invisible, the full-flecked irises, bathed in greenish light, shifting and shimmering with a naked rancour, like weed beneath the surface of a muddy pool. "José was taken yesterday to the *cuartel* . . . for stealing from your father."

As though the man had struck him, Nicholas shrank back, lost his balance, and actually fell from the wall.

"No . . . no," he whispered, scrambling to his knees.

"It is true," Garcia declared in an indiscribable tone, a whisper almost, yet so sinister it froze the child's heart. "He is in prison. Five years they will give him, at the least. Your José is a thief." His voice rose, he flung out his chest and with clenched fist thumped himself fiercely as though beating on a drum. "Don't get in Garcia's way. It is not wise. He will vanquish you. A man amongst men. A king upon his throne. Let all who hear take warning."

He stood a moment, his head thrown back, outlined against the opalescent sky; then, without further speech, he darted towards Nicholas a furtive glance, shot with a hidden threat, then turned and went off.

As though turned into stone, yet with a fierce throbbing in his chest, Nicholas remained motionless, lost and abandoned to despair. Now, indeed, he could understand his father's indulgence, the Professor's arch complaisance, Garcia's exalted mood . . . the pattern of the morning was complete. José in prison . . . a thief . . . oh, no, never, never, he thought, with a rending of his breast, never would they make him believe it. Small and useless though he might be, at least he would hold fast. They would never make him lose faith in his friend.

The sound of voices disturbed him, caused him to spin

130

round and peer across the wall. Two men were coming down the lane towards the villa. They came slowly, for they were old, both dressed in black with dusty boots, hobbling along like a pair of aged, bedraggled crows. The taller carried a faded black umbrella and wore a long *soutane*, and Nicholas made out, with a stifled cry of surprise, that he was a priest. Suddenly the little boy jumped up. He saw now, quite plainly, that the second old man was Pedro. Instinctively, he started to run and, skirting the formal garden, taking care not to be observed, he broke through the shrubbery in time to meet the two visitors in the drive.

"Pedro," he panted. "How are you? How is José? What are you doing here?"

The old man made a gesture, grave and sorrowful, with his hand.

"We are calling upon your worthy father."

"But why, Pedro? Oh, tell me, where is José?"

The priest had walked on slowly, limping a little, leaning on the old umbrella. Pedro glanced towards him, answered hurriedly:

"It is not wise that I talk to you, Nicco. It compromises our position. Things are extremely bad. But I pray God they may be better." Again he looked ahead and added, in a hasty undertone: "Take this, little *amigo*. Do not say a word."

He thrust a screw of paper into the boy's hot hand, then the next minute had rejoined his companion and was advancing towards the door.

In a flash Nicholas darted back into the bushes. Crouching unseen, with pounding heart, he opened the paper.

Dear Nicco,—I hope this may reach you. They have shut me up in the cuartel. *Is it not a joke? I can't say I am crazy about this place. To obtain exercise I am obliged to stand on my head. But it makes little difference. I shall soon be out, and we shall laugh together at whoever has made this great mistake. Should you have the opportunity, please water the new plants. Also it is better if you keep away from Garcia. Be of good*

131

cheer, amigo. *We shall yet go fishing again. I think it better if you destroy this note.*

Your friend,
José.

Nicholas read the letter three times, then, with glistening eyes, he placed it between his teeth and tore it into tiny shreds which, with a constriction of his throat, he bravely swallowed. Then, peering through the bushes to ascertain if he might come out safely, he saw, with a twinge of pain, that Pedro and the priest had not been admitted to the house. Instead, Garcia had thought fit to keep them standing at the door and now, coldly frowning, the Consul had appeared to interview them on the portico.

For a moment Nicholas watched the scene, then, conquering his fear, he crept on his hands and knees, scratching them badly but not minding in the least, through the shrubbery until he was near enough to hear.

"We are sorry to intrude upon you, *señor*," Pedro was saying in a tone of such humility it made the boy's heart bleed. "We know that your time is occupied by affairs of the highest importance. . . ."

"I am, indeed, extremely busy," the Consul snapped.

"That is what I say, *señor*. Nevertheless, the matter upon which we venture to approach you is of much importance to us. I myself am a poor and ignorant man. Perhaps I would not dare to come alone. But Father Limaza has been kind enough to promise that he will speak for me."

"Pray come to the point."

Nicholas could scarcely bear it. Parting the bushes, he made out his father, towering above him, strangely magnified, and Pedro, his withered cheeks quite pale, pressing his hands nervously together, as though in supplication.

"It is José, *señor*, my grandson. You are aware that he is in serious trouble."

The Consul moved impatiently, with a restive lift of his fleshy chin.

132

"Naturally I am aware of it. The matter is out of my hands. Why don't you go to the police?"

"Poor people have little influence with the police, señor. But if you, with your high position, were to speak one word . . ."

"I have no power to interfere with the course of justice, nor any desire to do so. Your grandson must suffer the consequences of his own act."

"But, señor . . . his act," Pedro stammered. "That is just what we cannot understand . . ."

"José is a good boy, señor." It was Father Limaza who spoke at last, in a quiet and pacifying tone. "I can assure you of that, and I have known him all his life."

Thrilled by these words of intercession, Nicholas, craning his little neck upwards, could just see the spare, bowed figure of José's champion. Then his heart sank. The old priest, draped in his rusty soutane, spotted in front with food-stains, clutching the ridiculous umbrella, his heavy, solid boots cracked in the uppers and foul with dried mud, seemed a sorry advocate indeed. His simple face, yellow and wrinkled, was marred by a purplish growth that sprang from the corner of his lips and which, by causing him to talk from the other side of his mouth, slurred his speech to the point of absurdity.

"It was I who baptised him, señor . . . gave him his first Communion . . . administered Confirmation. . . ."

The triteness of these words, uttered by such a scarecrow, actually infuriated the Consul.

"Most touching," he sneered with heavy sarcasm. "You seem to have prepared him admirably for a life of crime."

"Of course, we are all sinners." The old priest took not the least offence, nor did his gentle gaze stir from the Consul's face. "Yet I cannot conceive that José is a thief."

"Then my jewellery has simply vanished into thin air?"

"It is not impossible, señor. Stranger things have happened under Heaven."

"What a pity Heaven permitted the cuff-links to remain in his pocket."

133

"Ah, yes, *señor*; that is a damaging fact. But José maintains he did not place them there."

Harrington Brande smiled with haughty bitterness.

"He will find it difficult to convince the judge."

"No doubt, *señor*. But we are not his judges." He paused as though offering himself, and all his humble experience, with supreme simplicity. "I do not believe that José is guilty. But even if he were . . . if he had done this bad and stupid thing . . . would it not be an act of charity to forgive him?"

"Do you take me for a fool?" Brande answered harshly, moved to unexpected vindictiveness by this old idiot's attitude. "The articles he stole from me are extremely valuable. Several things . . . my sapphire ring . . . the watch I got from the Swiss Ambassador, to mention only two of them . . . are quite irreplaceable. Am I to let myself be robbed of these without a word?"

"Naturally, *señor*, your loss would be great. But would not the loss of a human soul be greater still? I have told you I know José. If he is sent to prison . . . he who loves the freedom of the open air . . . I will not answer for what might come of him . . . in his bitterness. . . ."

"That is no concern of mine."

"And again, *señor*," persisted the old priest, undeterred, with the gentle conciliation he might have used to persuade a stubborn child. "There are others to consider . . . weak and defenceless creatures, who, although unquestionably innocent, would, if you do not relent, be plunged into sorrow and want. You are aware that José supports his sisters . . . and my good friend, Pedro. . . ."

"Then your good friend Pedro must now work for himself," the Consul interrupted cruelly. "If his purpose in coming here was to perpetuate himself in idleness, I must tell you it has failed."

There was an immediate pause. Pedro, with bowed head, a deep flush spreading round his wrinkled neck, mumbled to his companion:

"What is the use? . . . Let us go."

134

Father Limaza's gentle eyes were sombre. He drew himself up, as though summoning a final effort from his very soul.

"I ask you, *señor*, for the last time, to be generous. As you expect it from above, do not be parsimonious of mercy to us. Pride is such a poor illusion. Are we not all of us suspended in the will of God? In the name of that God, withdraw your charge against José. If you do not, I fear that grave evil will come of it."

"I refuse," the Consul answered brutally.

A mortal silence followed. Then, from the old priest, a profound sigh. Nicholas, cowering in the bushes, could bear to gaze no longer. With tightly shut fists pressed against his eyes, he sank down in the dank earth, fighting, fighting to stifle his sobs. Blind and almost senseless, like a bird caught in a snare, he still heard the sharp slam of the door as his father returned to the house. Then, slowly, heavily, as though treading a measure of sadness, of inexorable pain, came the crunch of boots, the dragging of a lame leg, upon the gravel as the two old men retreated down the drive.

EIGHTEEN

THREE DAYS LATER Professor Halevy departed for Paris. In the full flow of his gratitude, the Consul insisted that his friend be spared the discomforts of the first stage of the journey—Garcia would drive him to Barcelona. As the two stood together in the hall, while the motor purred outside, Brande clasped the psychologist's hand in a sudden access of emotionalism.

"My dear Halevy . . . what can one say in appreciation of your invaluable aid?" He increased the pressure of his fingers. "You have been my support . . . my standby. . . ."

The Professor barely smiled. In the light of morning his slight figure, shrouded by the dark cape, seemed more

135

shrunken than ever, and his grey face, with its sharp-drawn features and blue pouches beneath the eyes, had the look of a hungry rodent.

"As a scientist I seek no thanks." His tone was studied; he toyed with the black chain which bound his cape. "Nevertheless, as your friend, I am gratified that my results should have been so exceptional. In my last two sessions with your son I have observed a definite reduction of the fixation. And when this fellow is out of the way the whole foundation of the complex should crumble and disappear." He shot a shrewd and stealthy glance at the other. "At the same time . . . I would ask you to be mindful of your own health."

"My health?" Brande repeated in surprise.

"You have permitted this affair . . . this Spanish youth . . . to over-excite you. Your reflexes are exaggerated, your nervous system is on edge."

"Oh, come now, dear friend." The Consul laughed, a trifle loudly. "Your affection for me makes you too anxious. I have never felt better in my life."

"No doubt. Revenge is a stimulating passion. But it may be dearly bought. Do not let it run away with you. For you . . . moderation is the only course." Halevy spoke with acid dryness, and started towards the door. "Ah, well . . . we shall see you in Paris one of these days." With an enigmatic, slightly sour smile, that pinched, impossible smile which exposed his pale gums almost in a sneer, he added: "No doubt when your book is published."

When the car drove off Brande remained standing upon the portico. In his present mood he would have preferred a more intense leave-taking, but Halevy, unpredictable, could, when he willed it, stifle all sensibility by his sterile and dispassionate detachment. Yet was there not a virtue in such firmness? It seemed so to the Consul at this moment. He had meant to go upstairs to see Nicholas before leaving for the office, but now, with a compression of his lips, he decided against such an overture. After all, it was not his place to break the estrangement—the boy must weaken first and come

136

running back, with open arms and pleading eyes, to him. Straightening his shoulders, he picked up his hat and stick, then set out on foot towards the town.

The morning was pleasant, the sun had not yet attained its full radiance and the Consul was in the mood for active movement. As he strode along he was conscious, within himself, of a deep, pervading sense of power. A heady distillate seemed flowing in his veins, pulsing through his body, mounting upwards to his brain in warm, dark waves. Behind that grave countenance, that staid composure, there worked a ferment more potent than wine. Like a lover tasting in advance the fulfilment of desire, he knew, and slowly savoured, a strange passion, the bitter-sweet intoxication of his hatred.

At the Consulate he went directly to his own room. He had no sooner seated himself at his desk when Fernando, the chief Spanish clerk, knocked and entered.

"Mr. Burton has gone to Porto Alijo, sir. In connection with the cargo of the *Eastern Star*. He was most anxious to speak with you, sir."

"Did he leave a message?"

"No, sir. He said he would return by five o'clock this evening. He indicated that it was most important."

"Important?"

"Yes, sir. . . . Mr. Burton seemed much disturbed."

"Very well," said the Consul brusquely. "He can see me when he gets back."

"And another matter, sir." The young Spaniard hesitated, dropped his full, coffee-coloured eyes. "They telephoned you at nine o'clock from the *corte*. It is decided that José Santero must go to Barcelona for trial. He will be taken there on Wednesday by the afternoon train."

A tingling, electric wave passed along the Consul's nerves —this, more than anything, was the news he wished to hear. He had feared all along that the case would come before the town police court, where local sentiment might easily sway the magistrate in the prisoner's favour. But at the High

137

Court in Barcelona it was a different matter. There the judgments were correct and strict, the sentences noticeably severe. With the greatest difficulty, Brande maintained his official air—his voice was slightly unsteady as he answered:

"Thank you, Fernando. That will be all."

When the clerk bowed and went out, the Consul's indifference left him; he rose impetuously and began to pace the strip of woven matting which ran the length of the narrow room. That dark gratification, burning more fiercely in his breast, would not permit him to be still. The thought of his approaching revenge grew and grew within him, until it suffused his every fibre. With hands locked behind his back, head bent forward, eyes bent staringly upon the floor, he moved to and fro, like a caged animal. He must, of course, be present at the trial to prefer the charges—already the scene in the court-room was vividly before his sight. But more than that, he would travel to Barcelona in the same train as the prisoner, sit near him in the compartment, witness at first hand every moment of his suffering, his shame. . . .

There was little work upon the Consul's desk: a tray of visa documents, some invoices of dutiable merchandise for export, his quarterly report on the commerce of the port; even so, he could not settle to it. The fever of restlessness was rising higher and still higher in his blood. He signed a few certificates, saw briefly two seamen who for the past hour had been waiting upon him to have their papers cleared, then went out early to the Café Chantaco for lunch.

His normal habit was to eat sparingly at midday, sometimes to have no more than a cup of coffee, but to-day he felt unusually sharp-set. Seated in a corner by the window, he ordered beefsteak, a savoury pimento omelette and some goat's-milk cheese, then, although he rarely touched liquor during the day, he drank in quick succession three glasses of *manzanilla*. A group of fishing skippers sat at an adjoining table with the pilot of the port, drinking beer, eating sardines and olives. Their deferential greeting increased his sense of personal authority, of manly physical power. At the back of

138

the bar someone was playing a concertina, a slow Catalan *cancion*, and the words, imbued with a haunting melody all in the minor key, falling and fading, mingling in his head with the native spirit, aroused and enticed him.

Lighting a cigar, for a while he made pretence of reading the *Voz de Madrid*, flicking the greasy pages over the wooden stick. But it was no use. He got up, threw a bill on the table, and left the café. Without purpose, he walked past the deserted, sun-bleached quays quivering in the afternoon glare, the thinly piled barrels emitting a hot odour of oil and resin. A phrase which Halevy had murmured one evening, with a deprecating shrug, kept echoing and re-echoing in his ear.

"My dear friend . . . a man of your virility, in the prime of life . . . assuredly, you surprise me."

Quite suddenly, as though driven by an inner force, he pulled down the brim of his hat and turned into the town, to a strange street, deserted at this hour, yet slightly sinister, then through a dark *patio*, to the arcaded corridor within. . . .

It was almost five o'clock when he got back to the Consulate and, with an inscrutable expression on his hard, pale face, went directly to his own room. On his passage through the outer office he observed, from the corner of his eye, that Alvin had already returned. Indeed, the assistant had been awaiting his chief with an expression of more than usual anxiety. He kept straightening his tie, with a characteristic gesture, and from time to time bent down in an effort to slap from his trousers turn-ups a powdering of meal dust picked up in the hold of the *Eastern Star*.

Brande sat down heavily in his swivel chair and, fumbling for his handkerchief, wiped the moisture from his brow. With the cambric square still in his hand he stared straight ahead for several minutes. His physical exhaustion had brought him some respite; nevertheless, he was angry at himself for his senseless adventure, and unaccountably depressed. At last, however, with a shrug he recovered himself, straightened his shoulders, abruptly rang the bell on his desk.

139

Immediately Alvin entered. The Consul, almost wooden in his seat, gazed at his assistant with a queer fixity.

"Well?" Brande spoke at last. "What is the matter?"

The Chief's manner had the effect of increasing young Burton's agitation.

"I'm sorry to have to worry you, sir. Really I am. But the fact is, I've had a letter from the agency."

"What agency?"

"The domestic agency," Alvin answered. "Oh, I assure you, sir, I did all I could ... wrote to the best place in Madrid. I wanted so much to please you, but I'm not really up to that sort of thing."

"Will you have the goodness to explain what on earth you are talking about?"

Alvin moistened his dry lips.

"It's your butler, sir ... Garcia ... the man I engaged for you. He had the highest references, and now the head of the agency has written me in confidence to say there's reason to believe these testimonials were forged. He says also that the authorities are looking for a certain man ... Rodrigo Espantago is his name ... and the agency thinks it may be Garcia. He's wanted for robbery with violence, and desertion from the Army. He broke out of a criminal mental asylum in Malaga where he was under observation. . . ."

Behind the impersonal mask of his authority Brande experienced a sudden, frightening stab. He had expected some petty official difficulty to be brought before him, the kind of legal misgiving which usually plagued Alvin's scrupulous mind. But this . . . this was something incredibly, fantastically different.

"Show me the letter," he said after a strangely rigid pause.

When Burton handed him the sheet, he read it through twice, sat for some minutes in heavy, fretful thought, then slowly raised his eyes to the assistant.

"There is nothing definite here. They offer no proof whatsoever."

"No, sir," agreed Alvin, earnestly. "But it all looks

140

fearfully suspicious. I talked it over with Carol and she was frightfully upset . . . begged me to come to you at once. Don't you think, under the circumstances, you should take some steps?"

Harrington Brande's pale lip curled.

"Are you . . . and your esteemed wife . . . instructing me as to what I should do?"

"Oh, no, sir," Alvin protested with a quick flush. "But this . . . this fellow seems such a dangerous character . . . and if he *should* be your butler . . ."

Again the Consul was conscious of a piercing thrust. Yet, in a coldly level tone, he answered:

"Garcia has been in my household for several months now. I have, at close quarters, had ample opportunity to study him. And I will say outright that I have never had a better or more trustworthy servant. In short, I regard this letter as wholly inapplicable. It's obviously a circular sent out by the agency to all their clients."

"But surely, sir," Alvin exclaimed, with great sincerity, driven from his habitual diffidence, "you will make some inquiry? I feel my own responsibility acutely."

"I think you may be assured that I shall do precisely what is needful"—the laboured irony twitched the Consul's cheek —"if only to relieve you of your weighty burden of anxiety." He folded the sheet carefully and placed it in his waistcoat pocket. "You will, of course, say nothing of this letter to anyone. Any such breach of confidence I should regard in a most serious light."

"Yes, sir," Alvin acquiesced in a subdued manner, yet darting a queer glance towards his chief. "You may depend on me."

"I trust so," said Brande in a pained voice. Rising from his chair, he put on his hat, paused a moment in secret hesitation at the door of his room, then turned and went out, his steps sounding heavy yet hollow upon the wooden stairs.

141

NINETEEN

EARLIER THAT AFTERNOON, lying fully dressed in his room, a sudden intensification of his heartsickness had swept over Nicholas. This separation from José was not to be borne. Was there nothing he could do to end it?

He knew that Professor Halevy had gone, relieving him at last of the misery of these questionings which, though he could not grasp their purpose, sent always a quick shame into his cheeks. And Garcia was away, driving the car to Barcelona, while Magdalena, more secretive, more unapproachable than ever, kept herself apart in her own quarters.

The deadly stillness of the house, petrifying though it was to his childish spirit, was at least an incentive to action. He got up, went into the garden, so sadly empty of life and movement, and, after a moment's throbbing indecision, gathered all his forces and set out along the coast road towards the town. At least it afforded him relief to put his limbs in motion and to have, at the back of his mind, some semblance of a purpose.

It was intensely hot, the sun, a dirty orange, beat down on him ferociously, and the way, which he had never walked before, now seemed interminable. When he reached San Jorge, quite tired out, he paused irresolutely. The dusty and deserted Plaza lay like a panting dog, the fronts of the houses, shuttered against the day, were like blind eyes, the narrow alleyways hoarded their shadows in secret.

Daunted, but not defeated, Nicholas made his way bravely across the square to the barrack ground, where the gaol was situated. But, alas! there, too, he halted, crushed suddenly by the formidable aspect of the prison, which stood squat and crenellated, flanked by twin towers, with a massive archway and rusted iron portcullis. The place was the old fortress of the town and, chilled by its blank façade and

142

gloomy depths, by the floating vulture which cast its broad winged shadow over it, the child felt his heart sink. His naïve idea of finding some loophole through which he might speak with his friend faded and died within him.

For some time he hung about, keeping his distance, in a timid fashion, hoping that some fortunate circumstance might arise to aid him. But nothing happened, nothing—it was as though no life of any kind existed behind these barred and stony walls. And suddenly, overcome by an access of panic, Nicholas took to his heels and bolted from the barrack square.

If he had been alarmed before, now he was desperately scared, and as he fled he had the awful fancy that the tall towers behind were reaching out long arms in an effort to entrap him. In his haste and terror he lost his way in a maze of little crooked lanes, a man in a black sombrero shouted after him, he almost fell over the figure of an old woman, a water-carrier, reclining on the pavement with her clay pitchers beside her.

Presently, however, by a stroke of fortune, he found himself in one of the narrow but familiar streets leading to the river. From far off a clock struck three frail strokes, the cry of a vendor of lottery tickets, though heard faintly, further reassured him, and, a spark of confidence returning, he slowed his pace and turned towards the Calle Corriente. He found José's home quite easily. Still breathing fast, he took up a position on the opposite pavement and stared up at the top storey with bright, distracted eyes. He had not the courage to mount the winding stairs to the little apartment, yet surely, if he waited, some sign would be manifest to him.

He did wait, for more than an hour, while the sun sank from its zenith and the air began imperceptibly to cool, but not one member of José's family appeared. Then, as he was about to give up and move disconsolately away, he saw old Pedro come out of the passage leading to the house. He swallowed dryly and, after an instant of paralysis, darted across the street.

143

"Pedro!" he exclaimed. "It's me . . . Nicco. Have you any news?"

The old man drew up and directed towards Nicholas his sadly troubled gaze.

"There is news, Nicco." He shook his head slowly. "But it is not good. José is to stand trial in the High Court at Barcelona. I fear it will go hard with him there."

"Oh, Pedro!"

"Yes, it is a bad business for everyone." The old man sighed. "But worst of all for José."

"How is he?" The boy's voice shook.

"Not well. He does not take kindly to being enclosed. From his earliest days he has lived out of doors. And if they should shut him up for a long time . . ." Pedro broke off with a doleful, significant sigh.

There was a dismal pause.

"I wonder . . . does he ever speak of me?" Nicholas could barely articulate the words.

"Yes." Old Pedro nodded. "Every time I see him. He sends a friendly message. And bids me tell you that somehow he will get out of this."

"But, Pedro," Nicholas whispered huskily, "could that be possible?"

The old man glanced warily up and down the empty street, then, bending upon Nicholas an eye turned surprisingly penetrating, he said in a low tone:

"I should not tell you this, Nicco. But you love José as we do, and therefore you are one of us. Now, listen, my child, there is just one chance that José may escape the snare. If he goes to Barcelona he is lost; on that we are all agreed. Also, there is nothing to be done while he remains here, in the gaol. But on the journey to the city"—the old man lowered his voice to a whisper—"it is perhaps possible that something may occur. We do not hope greatly, but still, we hope. And if we should succeed, then José will make his way into the mountains, to that old mill-house where you went to fish with

144

him. There he can lie safely for many weeks till everything is passed over and forgotten."

A short, stifled breath broke from the little boy's chest, and his wan face lit up with a sudden gleam. The old mill-house, by the stream ... oh, what a perfect place for José to hide ... and he could see him there, visit him on some pretext. So glowing was the prospect he scarcely dared to think of it. He stood there, motionless, gazing intently up at Pedro's wrinkled face; then, all at once, he pressed the old man's arm with fierce intensity.

"Yes ... yes," he exclaimed fervently. "Tell him ... tell him he must do it." And, turning, he sped away, with parted lips, as though smiling to himself, cherishing some secret, heartening thought.

His tiredness forgotten, Nicholas ran all the way home, and it was fortunate that he did so, since his father arrived at the villa somewhat before his usual time. Garcia had returned too, and for a moment the boy was fearful that he might be questioned as to how he had employed the afternoon. But the Consul was in a mood more than ever preoccupied and withdrawn; they sat down to dinner together without incident, and Nicholas breathed again as the danger passed.

For the past week Brande had treated Nicholas with a kind of formal courtesy. His love for the boy deterred him, absolutely, from any form of severity. There were moments when, swept by an inordinate longing, he desired to clasp his son passionately in his arms. But his pride, his deep sense of the injury which he had sustained, forbade such a show of weakness. He must first reassert his position, repair the damage to his paternal prestige, before their former relationship, so dear to him, founded, indeed, upon the child's admiration and respect, could be restored.

To-night, however, from his heavy air, a new problem seemed to possess his mind and, beyond a few trite remarks, he did not speak to Nicholas. Instead, his attention seemed focused, strangely, upon Garcia, and several times, contrary to his custom, he addressed the man when he came in to serve them.

"You saw Professor Halevy off?"

"Yes, *señor*."

"Was his train on time?"

"Are these trains ever on time, *señor*?" The butler's face expressed a saturnine contempt and he postured, negligently, one hand lightly on his hip.

"No, I suppose not." Brande coloured slightly, as though sensing for the first time a vague familiarity in the man's manner. "But he did get away safely?"

"Undoubtedly, *señor*. Do I ever fail the *señor*? At eleven o'clock."

Nicholas could not quite fathom the meaning of these exceptional exchanges, yet they made him uncomfortable, and he was glad when a nod from his father dismissed him, gave him liberty to retire to his room and, while he undressed, to treasure in solitude that brave new hope which his conversation with Pedro had planted in his heart.

Downstairs, the Consul still sat at table, dallying interminably with his port, revolving the glass between fretful fingers as though consumed by a crisis of indecision. Twice the butler had opened the pantry door to see if he might clear away, yet Brande had not moved. At the third appearance, however, the Consul suddenly raised his head.

"Garcia," he exclaimed, and broke off.

"Yes, *señor*."

Under the butler's level stare, the brows raised in arch interrogation, yet the eyes so expressionless as to be almost inhuman, Brande felt himself flinch. For the first time he sensed in that opaque gaze a vague derision masquerading as servility. Was it true, then, what Nicholas had so often and so timorously asserted? A flood of doubts, of suspicions, hitherto undreamed of, rushed into the Consul's mind, sending a deeper wave of confusion across his beset and brooding brow.

"Garcia," he said again resolutely, "I wish to speak with you."

The man bowed, too low by far, the very caricature of an obeisance. Brande gritted his teeth.

"When did you arrive back with the car?"

"At five o'clock, *señor*."

"But Professor Halevy left at eleven." Brande affected to consider. "Allowing two hours for your journey home, you should have been back at one."

Garcia's eyebrows lifted a trifle higher.

"One must eat, *señor*," he answered sardonically. "It was necessary for me to partake of a modest, a frugal repast."

"So you spent four hours over this modest repast?"

"I did not realise that there was need for haste. And I found it pleasant to prolong my luncheon."

"Did you drink during this prolonged luncheon?"

"*Señor?*"

"I have been watching you carefully during the past hour. It occurred to me that you had been drinking."

The butler's mouth drew down sharply at the corners. For a moment his look was deadly; then a glint of contemptuous mockery, of careless malice, flashed in the depths of his clouded eye.

"I am a human being, *señor*, and must take advantage of my opportunities. Frankly, I am accustomed to good wine. When I was with the Aosta family in Madrid I was served with the best marsala."

The Consul bit his lip sharply.

"You are very fond of referring to these Aostas. When were you with them?"

Garcia answered indifferently, with suppressed insolence:

"Some time ago."

"When?" repeated the Consul in a firmer tone.

Now indeed a perceptible change came into the butler's hooded eyes, a filming of the pupils, as though mud had been stirred up in their depths, creating a screen beyond which one could not penetrate.

147

"It is written in my papers," he said slowly. "They are all in order."

"Of course," said the Consul in a strange voice. He paused for an instant. "And you have never heard of an individual named Rodrigo Espantago?"

The butler's fleshy eyelids flickered once. His features, graven to immobility, seemed to solidify. There was a strange thickness in his voice as he replied:

"Why should I know of such a one? Who is he?"

"A criminal," Brande answered, "wanted by the Madrid police."

A bar of silence throbbed within the room. Garcia's face was deeply congested, his nose and cheeks suffused by a fine reticulation of purple veins. And suddenly he burst out, incoherently, through his swollen lips:

"Really, *señor*, I feel myself insulted. What do you think I am, to hurl such insinuations at my head? Is it my fault if I have made enemies? No, *señor*, a thousand times, no. And always I have found a way to confound them, these sneaking brutes." He was almost shouting now. "I spit upon them."

"Be quiet, Garcia," Brande exclaimed sternly, concealing his alarm.

"I am used to persecution," cried the butler, growing more and more excited. "I am a remarkable man. Often, when passing strangers in the street, I have heard them murmur: 'He is distinguished . . . of noble blood.' Bah! It is nothing. I am not proud. But am I responsible for the envy I excite amongst these others? There must be an end to it some day. Otherwise life becomes impossible. No man can continue to give everything and receive nothing. A meaningless sacrifice to which I will never submit. . . ."

"That will do."

Brande, in his concern, half rose from the table, but suddenly the butler's eyes were emptied of all light. A slight shiver, almost a convulsion, passed over him. He breathed heavily, then drew the back of his hand across his lips to wipe away the white froth which had gathered there. A moment

148

later, he glanced sideways towards the Consul. His manner was calm again, obsequious and ingratiating, yet in his voice there hung a veiled and subtle menace:

"Obviously someone has been slandering me. But I think I have always given satisfaction. Is not that correct, *señor*?"

"Of course," the Consul muttered.

"I am glad you are satisfied, *señor*. In that case, it should be easy to forget these foolish notions. Surely you have already had enough trouble in your household?"

There was a pause. Brande drummed his fingers on the table, unsatisfied, resentful, and ill at ease, yet strangely unwilling to press the issue further. When he spoke the words came almost diffidently:

"You can assure me there is no truth in these . . . these suggestions?"

"None whatever, *señor*. Let your mind be at rest. I shall get more papers from Madrid. In a few days I can give you all the proof you require." Garcia showed his tobacco-stained teeth in a confiding, chilling smile. "And now, *señor*, have I your permission to clear the table?"

"Yes," said Brande heavily. "I have finished."

He went out of the room and slowly climbed the stairs, hesitated for a moment on the landing, then entered his bedroom, where he stood, staring ahead of him, in deep, tormented thought. It was enough, he told himself, that Garcia had denied the accusation. For his own part, he had not faltered in his duty, he had placed the matter squarely before the butler, questioned him closely, and been re-assured. What more was there to be done?

And yet, at the back of his mind, there lurked the horrible certainty that Garcia was indeed the man sought for by the police. His behaviour during the interview had been so strange—'unbalanced' was the only word which fitted it—and his last smile, placating yet cunning, so charged with baleful complicity it gave the lie to all his protestations, and fatally betrayed him.

Brande felt his head reel, like a mountain-climber who,

149

suddenly confronted by a precipice, is unable to advance or retreat. Yet advance he must, he had gone too far to draw back. All his forces were focused, concentrated now in flaming incandescence, upon the prosecution of José. Any steps which he might take against Garcia must delay, perhaps defeat, this main objective. No, no. Further investigation of Garcia must be postponed until José's case was settled. After all, the butler had promised to produce proofs of his identity within the next few days. It was only reasonable to afford him this short space of time to do so. Then, if everything was not in order, measures could be taken to secure his prompt removal.

Thus Brande argued, with frowning, feverish obstinacy, closing his mind to the fact that if Garcia should be all that was suspected of him, then José, almost certainly, was innocent. Blind and deaf to reason, he shut out all externals; the matter was settled, his final decision had been taken, and now he awaited the approaching moment of fulfilment.

TWENTY

WEDNESDAY CAME STILL and humid, filled with immense, opalescent sheets of light. Out of the grey and glassy sky a soft heat poured silently, in unseen waves which failed to stir even the thin, motionless leaves of the mimosa trees. The long fronds of the tamarisks fringing the lane hung limp and drooping like the tongues of thirsting beasts. Sounds travelled from afar, vibrated upon the ear, as from the strumming of some gigantic harp. At the Casa Breza the hum of the distant town was unnaturally clear, yet oddly muted. Only the rasping of the cicadas broke the inexorable stillness, insatiable, interminable.

This queer, impenetrable day seemed to match the Consul's mood, which, from the moment of his rising, was set and gloomy. Since he had taken his decision, two night before, he knew that there was no looking back, and his mind was firmly fixed upon what must inevitably come to pass. Yet his strange depression would not lift.

After breakfast, before departing for the office, he drew Nicholas aside into the embrasure of the salon, and with a kind of painful logic explained to him what he was forced to do. It eased him somewhat that the boy listened with proper docility, for he had feared the possibility of another outburst, a scene. Only when he was about to leave, as he stepped from the portico to the car, did Nicholas, standing at the front door, raise his bowed head.

"Don't go, Father." He spoke in a low voice, with only the faintest tremor of his lips.

"I must, Nicholas."

At that the boy suddenly gave way, and with a little rush, cried out:

"Father, I beg of you not to go. It is not necessary. Let them take José without you."

But Brande was by this time in the automobile. He raised a restraining hand, shook his head in reproof, and the next minute was gone.

At the office, during the forenoon, he studiously kept his thoughts away from the coming journey. Several intending immigrants had to be interviewed and their documents attested, after which a number of ship clearances demanded his attention, and when these had been disposed of he sat down to draft a letter to Restaud et Cie, a firm of Parisian publishers recommended by Halevy as being most likely to do justice to his work on Malbranche. His pen did not flow with its customary fluency and for some reason he felt sluggish, bound by a physical lethargy. Yet it gave him a momentary satisfaction to reflect that his manuscript was at last complete, parcelled in his bedroom, ready for the mail.

At one o'clock, shunning the public gaze of the Chantaco, he had a sandwich and a cup of coffee brought to his room; then, some twenty minutes later, he set out for the station. Rain had begun to fall, in large warm drops which left coin-

151

like splashes on the dusty pavements, yet the Consul walked slowly, unmindful of the wet. So rabidly had he anticipated this moment, this hour of justice, that he experienced, within himself, a strain of anger that his mood should be so listless and so dull. Of course, he had again been sleeping atrociously, and on the previous night had snatched barely an hour of fitful slumber. Yet this alone could not explain the change in him. Fantastic though it seemed, he had not yet shrugged off the recollection of his indiscretion—the word was his own—on that torrid afternoon, two days before. Nor could he banish from his mind that gnawing doubt of Garcia. Strive as he would, it kept creeping back upon him, shaking his pose of high integrity, infusing him with intolerable despondency.

At the station the party had already arrived—Pedro, José, and the *guardia*, sheltering together on the platform under the projecting roof of the *despacho de billetes*. The Consul looked at them heavily, observing with vague astonishment how gaunt and sallow José had become, how unkempt was his appearance, how closely the handcuffs forced him to stand beside the *guardia*. Viewing him after the interval of a week, Brande was conscious of no especial surge of his aversion, only a queer reluctance which increased as, having taken his ticket, he advanced towards the youth. He was like an automaton, compelled by forces which he himself had set in motion and which were now out of his control.

When he reached the little group, Pedro and José avoided his gaze, but the *guardia* saluted him briskly with his free hand.

"Wet, isn't it?" Brande remarked after a moment.

"Very wet, *señor*," the *guardia* answered briefly, yet respectfully.

There was a long pause during which the Consul's eyes kept straying to these shiny handcuffs. Somehow they provoked him to a strange distaste. The steel bracelet, he could see, had raised a weal upon the *guardia's* wrist. And suddenly he exclaimed, in a voice which, though irritated, remained aloof:

"Do you need these things?"

"Only until we are safely in the train, *señor*."

Again a heavy silence fell, broken by the drumming of the rain on the corrugated roof and the low mutter of voices from behind the barrier. Through the singular sense of fantasy that now enveloped him Brande became aware of the crowd that had gathered outside the *despacho*, of their hostile stares and vulgar imprecations. In a dignified manner, he averted his gaze. A moment later Pedro, detaching himself, shuffled off to buy a newspaper. When he returned he made, in an undertone, some remark to José concerning the weather. José did not answer. Fretfully, the Consul shifted his position. Would the train never come? This waiting was intolerable.

At last the air was rent by a shrill whistle, the pounding and screech of wheels. As the short train jerked to a stop, Brande moved forward with a feeling of relief and preceded the others into the single wooden compartment. There were few other passengers, mostly country people, a pair of travelling salesmen, some old women with baskets. It had been his intention to secure a position facing José, but something now withheld him. Instead, he seated himself a little distance away, at the top of the coach, before a spotted mirror advertising some liquid dentrifice. Thus, though his back was towards the group, he could see the dim reflection of what was taking place. Settling himself on the ribbed wooden bench, he prepared to endure the usual delay occasioned by the switching of the engine.

Finally, this was done and, with a start and a bump, they clattered off. Viewing the scene behind him, as the train picked up speed, Brande saw the *guardia* take a key from his pocket and unlock the handcuffs from José's wrist. The youth muttered a word of thanks and began to chafe the circulation into his hand. Pedro, with the paper before him, was reading aloud, apparently trying to interest the others in the sporting news. But neither gave him much attention. The *guardia*, sitting erect, maintained a correct official attitude, while José, with his face averted, stared steadily through the corridor at the fleeting, rain-drenched landscape.

That fixed and pensive profile, emptied of all gaiety, stamped with a new maturity, with a grave, personal dignity, began slowly, and in a most distressing manner, to affect the Consul. He ought, surely, to have rejoiced in this just retribution for the harm inflicted upon him. But he could not. The victory had suddenly become hollow, dust and ashes in his mouth. Studying José's image covertly in the mirror, he felt an extraordinary weakness creep over him. And he had a sudden impulse to go over to the youth, to speak to him kindly, to promise a measure of leniency. Yet how, in Heaven's name, could he do that now? The idea was nonsense. By a tremendous effort, the Consul wrenched his eyes away from the glass and, removing his hat, wiped with his handkerchief the perspiration which rimmed his brow.

The heat in the compartment was unbearably oppressive. Although the end door immediately in front of Brande was open, the rush of humid air which entered was like a furnace blast. In addition, he became aware that he had placed himself adjacent to the *comun*, the coach latrine which, on this line, was never maintained in a proper condition.

Yet he would not or could not change his position, but remained sunk into himself, gripped by a profound lethargy, while the atrocious train rattled and swayed over the uneven metals. From time to time someone pushed past him in the narrow aisle to enter the *comun*. The heavy grinding of the wheels came in bursts, exploding like surf against his eardrums, echoing and re-echoing through his head. Was he ill? Instinctively, he asked himself the question. But no, despite his febrile symptoms, he knew that his disorder was not physical. It was, if anything, an affliction of the spirit, an apprehension he could not name, fallen from he knew not where, weighing upon him with the imminence of doom.

The coast at this point of the journey became broken, indented by many inlets of the sea, and the railway, cutting inland, made a detour through the foothills of the mountains. Here, if anything, the sultry haze was thicker and, as in a

154

dream, trees, vineyards, and little white farmsteads, mistily obscured, flashed past the Consul's gaze. The track, badly laid, made no pretence of keeping to the level—at one minute the engine tore down a giddy slope while the next, gradually losing its momentum, it panted slowly to the succeeding summit.

In a kind of stupor, the Consul glanced at his watch. Not yet three o'clock. And they had come no more than fifteen kilometres from San Jorge. He groaned inwardly, realising how much longer this tribulation must endure, and almost furtively he raised his eyes towards the mirror. Yes, they were still sitting in silence, exactly as before. Yet as he peered, from beneath his brows, into the greenish speckled glass he saw José turn, quietly, and address a brief remark to the *guardia*. There was an instant's pause, then the *guardia* nodded assent, and made way for José to rise and pass into the aisle.

The Consul's heart gave a sudden, heavy bound. He saw, of course, that José had asked permission to go to the *comun*, and the sudden realisation that the youth was now approaching, must brush closely past him, was enough, in his complex state, to set his nerves a-quiver. Every cell in his body, reacting tensely, made him aware of José's steady advance. More and more he drew himself together, as if in dread of a violent blow. Yet, even while his flesh contracted, he knew it was not this he feared. No, deep in the dim recesses of his consciousness, there formed slowly, and floated upwards, the intuition, veiled yet terrifying, that the moment drawing near was to be, in some strange and tragic manner, a crisis in his destiny.

José, swaying with the motion of the compartment, was now close behind him. Brande could scarcely breathe. He tried to close his eyes, to feign sleep. Impossible. As though compelled by forces stronger than his will, he shifted his gaze and looked directly up at José.

The youth was now slightly in front of him, steadying himself against the end partition, waiting for a momentary

155

aggravation of the jolting to abate. His eyes, dark in his pale face, bore down upon the Consul, searchingly, inscrutably, yet without rancour. It seemed almost that a faint smile was hidden in their depths. Then, quietly, he turned his head away.

The train, having furiously rattled itself downhill to a little valley, was now met by a noticeably steep ascent. As its speed slackened, José took a calm step forward.

As he did so, in a lightning stroke of illumination the Consul guessed the youth's intention. He saw that José was not going into the cabinet, but, using this merely as a pretext, was about to jump through the open door of the coach. A sudden convulsion swept over Brande. Apathy fell from him, his breath swelled into his throat, choking him. He must not, he could not permit José to escape. It was dangerous, too, for him to leap from the moving train. Which of these thoughts were uppermost in the Consul's mind, then or later, he never knew. At that second, as José jumped, he leaned forward with an incoherent cry and tried to hold him. His hand clutching wildly, caught the selvedge of José's coat. The poor fabric ripped instantly, but the restraint, slight though it was, broke the force and power of José's spring. Deprived of his expected impetus, he lost his balance in mid air, and failed to land clear. Instead, his body sprawled forward and as he fell, by some fateful, pre-ordained design, his foot was firmly caught between the footboard and the framework of the coach, so that his head struck, downwards, with brutal force, upon the edged metals of the track.

Again the Consul gave out that inarticulate cry. Starting to his feet, he blundered forward, shouted for someone to stop the train. At once a commotion arose, hands tugged the emergency signal. In a daze of nausea, Brande heard the train brakes screech in anguish, felt the compartment shiver all over, then grindingly slow down. With a final hiss of steam the train slithered and grated to a standstill, an immobility which was somehow terrifying. Immediately everyone

156

crowded out of the coach, there was a rush of passengers back along the track. Completely alone, the Consul straightened himself in the empty compartment. He must go, he must. Dizzily, he made his way to the exit.

They had freed José. His body lay limp and extended on the green embankment. The clothing had been arranged. Someone had placed a clean handkerchief over the mutilated face. The grass, mountain grass, was soft and green, starred by little yellow flowers. A clear sound of running water reached the ear. It was not far from the river he had loved, the sanctuary he had hoped to attain.

Old Pedro, standing with the watchers, did not look at the Consul. But in a low voice, a broken whisper, he said:

"He will not go to prison now, *señor*."

TWENTY-ONE

IT WAS NEARLY ten o'clock that night before the Consul found himself, exhausted and dishevelled, on the sandy lane leading to the Casa Breza. Completely overcome, he had felt unable to travel back to San Jorge by train, and had walked away from the railway line, striding blindly across fields, ditches, and stone walls, heedless of his destination, bent only upon escaping from that fatal scene. After five o'clock he had stumbled into the tiny village of Offerino. Here, from the little post office in the general store, he had telephoned the Consulate. But there was no answer; the place was closed, they had all gone home. Next he had tried to get through to his house, meaning to ask Garcia to fetch him in the car. Yet again he failed: first the number did not answer, then it was engaged, and, finally, amidst the inevitable buzzing, was reported out of order.

Normally the inefficiency of the local system was a source of maddening irritation to Brande. Now, however, he left the dark cavern of the shop without a word. They told him that a bus would leave for San Jorge at eight o'clock. Silently, with bowed head and drooping shoulders he seated himself on a bench outside the whitewashed *fonda*, refused the innkeeper's courteous offer of refreshment and, unconscious of the curious glances of the tavern's patrons, simple country people, surrounded by their wagons and beasts, taking their refreshment in the open air, began passively to wait.

Sick, empty, and weak, he found it easy enough to let his weary limbs relax. But his brain, alas! was less quiescent, throbbing crazily, as if to split his skull, spinning an endless web of anguished thought. José dead, wiped out, his young life extinguished . . . it still seemed impossible to him; yet it was so, there was no escape from that irrevocable fact. Fixing his wandering and almost witless thoughts, he tried to reason that it was an accident . . . oh, a most regrettable accident, yet one which was quite unavoidable, which he indeed had done his utmost to prevent.

But wait . . . he must not rush, not quite so fast, to that comforting conclusion. Did no one hate José with a bitter, spiteful hatred, harass and persecute him, drive him to the brink? A soundless groan came from the Consul's lips, a cry of pain, unuttered, wrung from the depths of his being. The arrival of the bus broke only for a moment the torment of his thoughts, barely dispelled that vague reverie which filled his eyes with shadow. Stiffly he clambered into the narrow vehicle, which was almost empty, and sank into the corner with a heavy sigh. When they drove off darkness had begun to fall. His heart beat heavily as they drew near San Jorge.

Now, having left the bus at the head of the lane, he was suffused by an agitation so acute he scarcely dared approach the solitary house. With the advent of dusk the mist had vanished and a wind arisen. Now Brande could hear its muffled drumming through the low cedars on the cliff. It was as though the sky vibrated, stirred by the echoes of a gigantic bell. Ahead of him the path lost itself in the pitch blackness. Although he advanced slowly, the Consul felt out of breath; he had to clench his hands tight to force himself to go on.

Suddenly, amidst the indistinct masses of obscurity ahead, the moon came surging through the sea of sky and the outline of the villa loomed whitely before him. The wind, roaring spitefully up the drive, bit into him like a whiplash. A shutter banged loudly at the back premises. Bent double, his arms pressed against his sides, he took advantage of a short lull between two gusts to pass round the side of the house. In the sudden burst of moonlight the luminous shadows of the mimosa trees danced upon the gravel drive and their threadbare foliage was slit by silver blades. Then, all at once the moon went out, and the blackness was deeper, denser than before. Panting, he gained the shelter of the portico, paused for a moment, his head aslant, listening to the stillness, then, with desperate resolution, pushed open the door.

Inside, the hall was swimming with darkness, a great dark pool filled with the hollow thudding of his heart. Then he became aware of a strange odour, acrid and smoky, which stung his nostrils and drew the moisture to his eyes. Bewildered, he felt himself powerless, seeming to be surrounded by movement yet himself unable to move. This incomprehensible paralysis, which lasted only a few seconds, seemed prolonged for hours. The clang of the shutter freed him. His body emerged from torpor and, unsteadily, he lit a match. It flickered wanly between his shaking fingers, spluttered, and went out.

At that moment, above the howling of the wind, he heard the sound of weeping. Turning with a jerk, his head over one shoulder, he searched the darkness with strained intentness. The sobs continued. He groped his way towards the door of the kitchen and opened it before he succeeded in raising his eyelids. Magdalena was before him, seated at the table, rocking herself to and fro in a passion of despair.

"Magdalena," he said in a scarcely audible voice.

She looked towards him and he saw her face, disfigured

159

by a great purple weal, hollowed by terror, suddenly aged, unrecognisable.

"What . . ." he said, and broke off with a trembling of his shoulders.

Staring at him, as at an apparition, she clutched at her torn black bodice.

His voice came back to him.

"For God's sake . . . what is the matter?"

A pause, filled by the prowling of the wind without.

"He has gone," she moaned.

"Who has gone?"

"Garcia . . . after all that I have done for him. . . ." She gave way to little muffled cries that ended in a fit of coughing.

A thin spasm of anger threaded the Consul's apprehension. He went forward and shook her.

"Tell me quickly . . . where has he gone?"

Heads in hands, in a muddled fashion, she seemed to try to think, to remember.

"He has gone where you or any of the others will never find him. He can go fast in your splendid automobile. You will never find that either." As Brande started involuntarily, she raised her wounded eyes, kindled now by a spark of bitterness. "What did you expect, my fine master? That Rodrigo would wait until the police came to call upon him? Yes, that's his name, Rodrigo Espantago. He's a thief, a criminal, a maniac, all in one. He fooled you nicely, and me too, as he fools everyone. He's not my husband. I'm only his woman. Teamed up with him in Madrid. He promised me he'd treat me right. He got round me, got me to do all the work, to slave for him, the lazy, filthy devil . . . and now he's gone." Her voice, tortured, rose to a scream. "Why did you let him know that they were after him? If you had only heard him mock at you! At you and your little Professor. The stuffed codfish and the curried shrimp . . . that's what he called the pair of you. He planted everything on José. Didn't you guess that? He hated José and swore he'd send him to the *cuartel*. He hated Nicholas too. Meantime, he

160

had all your jewellery, a pretty lot of loot. And now . . ." She began to shake hysterically, torn between tears and a terrible rending laughter. "Now he's got more. He's done you down properly, like he always said he would. Just wait till you see. . . ."

Completely broken down, she swayed backwards and forwards, moaning to herself, arms folded over her breasts, features contorted, tears streaming down her cheeks. No persuasion, no amount of shaking could stir her.

Abruptly, Brande gave it up. He turned and lit the candle which stood upon the dresser, then, with a pale, desperate face, he left the kitchen, holding the flickering flame aloft. In the hall, shielding the light from the eddying draughts, he glanced round fearfully. Everything seemed in order. He began, slowly, to mount the stairs, with the regular steps of a somnambulist. Outside his own room he paused. The air felt cold and, besides the reek of melting tallow, was filled with that smoky odour which he had noticed earlier. As though overcoming a strong resistance, breasting an invisible barrier, he entered, and lit the gas.

The stark disorder of the bedroom struck him like a blow. All the drawers were pulled out, the floor was strewn with scattered garments, the wardrobe had been emptied of his best suits. The silver toilet articles were missing from the dressing-table, his heavy ivory brushes, the chased cigar box. The room had been stripped of everything of value, systematically and with wanton destructiveness. Yet this caused him no distress, barely disturbed the surface of his numbed sensibilities. He looked about him, with darting, hunted glances, then his eye struck downwards to the hearthstone and lit upon a charred and crumbled mass which lay there. At first he did not comprehend, then with a painful indrawing of his breath he bent forward. Yes, it was his manuscript, burnt to shreds, totally destroyed.

He gave a terrible sigh, a lost and gasping sound, straightened himself with that same pale, expressionless face, dusted the sooty fragments from his fingers. The frightful effort which he made to retain control of himself gave to each of his jerky movements a mechanical precision. This was his punishment, then, the loss of his life's work; it might be that he had deserved it. His mouth made an imperceptible grimace, as though gulping down hot tears. He stood for a moment, apparently in deep thought, actually in a state of blankness; then, like a child seeking consolation, he picked up the candle and turned towards his son's room.

A moment later, he was staring at the empty bed which had not been slept in. A blast of cold air made him spin round. The window was wide open at the foot. His heart beat against his breast in great heavy strokes. He felt his legs give way under him, but just saved himself from falling. He pressed his fingers against his eyeballs, withdrew them. But still the room was empty, the window open to the pitch-dark night. Then the cry which he had been forcing back all night burst from his throat. In abject terror, he staggered from the room and stumbled downstairs to the kitchen.

"My son." The words came in a raucous whisper. "Where is Nicholas?"

Magdalena had in part composed herself, but his reappearance caused a sulky anger to flash through the misery in her eyes, which glowered at him from beneath the malignant bruise.

"Where, indeed?" she said tauntingly. "Did you expect to find him sleeping peacefully . . . after that devil had rampaged through the house? . . ."

The Consul came close to her. Leaning a little to one side, holding on with all his strength, he looked as though he were about to lose his balance.

"Tell me," he shouted.

The housekeeper stirred sullenly. Then her gaze fell, beaten down by the naked torment in his leaden face.

"Garcia didn't touch him," she faltered. "He would have, but Nicholas had gone. This afternoon he made up a little bundle and ran away."

Brande twisted his tongue in his dry mouth.

162

"Where did he go?"

"How should I know?" Magdalena shot back bitterly, then, as though repenting: "When I saw him running down the drive I called him from the kitchen window. But he would not stop. 'I am in a hurry, Magdalena,' he called back to me. Then in a crazy sort of way, with his little face very white and desperate, he called again, 'I am going fishing.' "

At first he thought that she had lost her senses, but suddenly a gleam of understanding dawned upon him. From Halevy's probings he was aware of the child's excursion to Torrido, and the depth of the impression which it had left upon his mind. José's bid for liberty had clearly been premeditated. Nothing was more likely than that Nicholas, forewarned, had set out to meet his friend at that mountain stream.

Brande was taken by a swift downward sinking, the same sensation that he had experienced during that fatal moment upon the train, and at the same instant a vision rose before him of his son, lost amongst the high hills, wandering into the swollen torrent, the roaring waters closing over him, in the pitch blackness of this stormy night.

As though to reinforce this image, a heavy gust of wind banged the shutter again, and a spatter of rain rattled like nails against the window panes. He felt his muscles relax, a rasping in his throat, a suffocation in his chest. Then, with a supreme effort, he collected himself, plunged back into the hall.

Never more than at this moment had he felt the utter loneliness of his position in the world. To whom could he turn in his frightful hour of need? Only one name rose feebly to his mind, that of the humble, disparaged Burton, whose advice he had so cynically rejected only a few days before. But now he clutched at his solitary hope. Groping for the telephone receiver, he asked for the number, gasped with relief when Alvin's voice came through to him, then, in a

163

desperate rush of words, begged his assistant to come at once, with a car.

Waiting, bareheaded, in the rain-swept portico, he lost all count of time. Yet it was not long before the sharp whine of a motor cut across the moaning of the wind, and a taxi-cab screeched at high speed round the curve of the drive and slithered to rest on the sodden gravel. Immediately Brande stumbled towards it, tugged open the door and, with heavy awkwardness, fell inside.

"Tell him," he mumbled, "tell him to drive to Torrido."

The taxi ran down to the stables, reversed noisily in the yard, then sped back along the lane. In the cramped interior darkness of the cab, swayed by an invisible swell, the Consul lay back, annihilated by a physical pain which pressed like lead upon the nape of his neck. Dimly he sensed that Burton had heard the news of José's death but did not dare to speak of it. Indeed, it seemed as though Alvin could not find any words to break the silence. But at last he stammered:

"I was lucky to pick up a cab at the station." A pause. "I hope you're all right, sir?"

Brande did not answer. Huddled in the narrow seat, he made a forward gesture with his arm, demanding greater and still greater speed. Then, in a husky voice, he muttered:

"Faster . . . faster . . ." After a long pause, he added, as if speaking to himself, "I am looking for my son."

"Nicholas?" exclaimed Alvin, in subdued surprise. "Is he at Torrido?"

"He left to go there this afternoon. Whether he has arrived . . . I do not know."

"We shall find him, sir," Alvin said consolingly. "Please don't worry."

This encouragement sent a tremor across the Consul's cheek, a stab into his bursting heart. He turned to Alvin and, pressing his hand, he sought to justify himself. "I did not mean it, Burton . . . before God, I did not mean it." Then, as the young man looked at him, uncomprehending and aghast, he bent forward, his chin almost resting on his knees, and

164

peered through the rain-streaked window of the cab, searching the road with straining eyes.

Now they had left the main coastal thoroughfare and were on the secondary country road, beginning the long and winding climb into the mountains. At every curve the car skidded on the muddy surface, then shuddered in all its members as the wheels gripped and the engine picked up again. The lowest gear kept up a constant drone, while in front the headlights sent two faded yellow beams which barely illuminated the dreary and deserted track.

On they went. Once Alvin let out a sharp exclamation, and Brande's heart stirred with hope, as they discerned a moving form ahead of them. But it was only a benighted farm labourer, plodding back to his homestead in the valley. Apart from that solitary figure, they might have been traversing the country of the dead.

At last, through the pelting downpour, a few faint lights glistened on the summit, like beacons upon a misty sea.

"Torrido," said the driver. Five minutes later, with a grunt of relief, he drew up in the deserted square.

"Why do you stop?" cried the Consul.

"The *señor* wished to go to Torrido." The driver spoke shortly. "We are there."

"Go on," said Brande.

"Should we not make some inquiries here?" Alvin suggested diplomatically. He glanced at the luminous dial of his watch, which showed five minutes past eleven. "It's very late."

"Go on," the Consul repeated in an indescribable tone. With a surly shrug, the driver threw in the gears, the car rasped forward, through the little village, on to the murky plateau beyond.

The road, washed out in places by the floods, was now difficult, almost impassable, and the cab proceeded at a snail's pace for a distance of nearly half a kilometre. Still nothing was visible on the narrow way. The driver, glancing back at Burton, was about to raise a final protest when

165

suddenly the silent darkness was enlivened by a sound, a movement, and all at once the shafts of light, wavering ahead, caught and held prisoner a small figure, tramping forward on the far side of the track

"My God!" Alvin cried. "It's Nicholas."

The Consul stared through the window like a lunatic. So positive was his belief that he would never see his son alive that the shock almost deprived him of his reason. A great shiver traversed his frame, his jaw began to chatter, the eyeballs protruded from beneath his forehead. No, no . . . it was no illusion . . . there was his beloved child, facing the car, blinking in pale inquiry under the headlights, his knapsack across his shoulder, drenched and bedraggled, as he might well be, but safe . . . oh, yes, dear Heaven . . . safe and sound.

A shout burst from the depths of the Consul's breast, broken and incoherent, abject, triumphant, a wild inhuman cry. He thrust open the door, hurled himself from the car.

"Nicholas," he wept, stumbling forward. "My son . . . my son."

TWENTY-TWO

SEVEN MONTHS LATER, on a clear, cold winter evening, the steamer from Stockholm passed up the Norlanger Fjord and with two short, cheerful blasts of its siren approached the Swedish port of Halversholm. Immediately the sturdy little vessel docked, its handful of well-wrapped passengers disembarked and although, purposely, the new Consul had given no notice in advance, he was met by a short, bearded, bustling man in a blue pilot coat, who introduced himself as the Harbour-master, Mr. Andersen, explaining with a genial smile that he had received advice of the arrival of Mr. Brande and his son from the shipping company.

The town lay already deeply under snow, the sky gleamed

166

with myriads of stars, sharp and shining as a dust of brilliants, the northern wind which scoured round the customs house was keen and invigorating. Andersen, in a jolly, hospitable fashion, with a tinge also of native inquisitiveness, proposed to take the newcomers to his house for supper, but the Consul hastily explained that they had partaken of dinner on the boat, that his son, who had just recovered from a protracted illness, was overtired, that they desired nothing more than to take possession of their new residence.

The Consulate, towards which Andersen agreeably conducted them, was quite near, a narrow-fronted house in a grey-stone terrace, opening directly on the broad, snowbound stretch of the Reivplatz, not more than a few hundred paces from the end of the wharf. It was a modest dwelling, made somewhat ridiculous by its steeply pitched roof and gabled dormer windows, but it looked solid and compact, with the living quarters above and the offices—to which access was obtained through a railed-off side entrance—upon the ground floor immediately below.

No one was at hand but a very old watchman, puffing his meerschaum in the basement beside a big porcelain stove, and Andersen insisted heartily that he must send his wife to see them settled for the night. They might need fresh milk, or fuel, or extra blankets—Mrs. Andersen had two fine spare eiderdowns she would be most happy to bring over. The Consul, however, was firm in his refusal. A rapid, if weary, glance showed him that these apartments, although far from spacious, were clean and habitable. The bedrooms were in order, linen and towels had been freshly laid out. He assured the Harbour-master that he and his son were old campaigners, thanked him for his offer to provide a hot breakfast—a real Swedish breakfast, Andersen volubly declared—in the morning, saw him to the front door, and finally got rid of him.

As the Consul turned and began to climb the scrubbed pinewood stairs, he was suddenly conscious of his own tiredness, and he realised with a pang how these last few months

167

had slowed him down. He felt older, much older, his shoulders were thickened by a stoop far heavier than he would have owned to before, his hair, in need of trimming at the back of the neck, was shot with grey, and his features, no longer sustained by that heavy, fleshy chin, showed a queer gauntness. To-night, at least, physical stress had banished the arrogance from his eye, his expression was resigned, even careworn. Yet he was relieved to be here, in the obscurity of this small, 'single-handed' berth—without doubt Bailey, whom he had once maligned, had done him some service in proposing his transfer, in promoting Alvin Burton to his place. The feeling against him at San Jorge had been acute. And Nicholas, although recovering physically, had failed, excusably, to shake off his melancholy lassitude in an environment which brought every day poignant reminders of the past. Perhaps, here, amongst these glittering northern snows, so different from the parched Iberian heathlands, life would be better for both of them ... at least for Nicholas ... he wanted nothing for himself.

Yes, he reflected sombrely—feeling himself more than ever a homeric figure, beaten and broken, yet bravely supporting the blows which Fate had delivered at him—his ambition must henceforth be sacrificed to the welfare of his son. Indeed, he drew sweet consolation from the prospect of his arid destiny. The edifice of his pride, though shattered, was not wholly destroyed, and from the noble ruins had sprouted this exquisite flower of martyrdom. From now on he would be content 'to jog along' ... towards 'the evening of his life'—these phrases were his own, already current in his conversation, the password, so to speak, of the days to come. Even the thought of the great work on Malbranche failed to rouse him. Already, with a kind of pathetic grandeur, he viewed himself as a new Carlyle, his life work ruined by a vicious servant, but, unlike that other historian, the circumstances of his existence, the tragic personal drama which had so profoundly affected him, forbade him to recreate it.

Upstairs, the boy was already in bed, his eyes closed, the

168

white coverlet drawn up to his chin. In him, the change was even more apparent. He was much taller. His legs stretched out long and lanky, his features had lost their babyish curves, were cast in a more masculine mould—he seemed to have gained the firmness which his father had lost. Gazing at him with a sort of hungry concentration, the Consul thought again, with an inward sigh: he is growing up.

"You are not asleep, Nicholas?"

"No, Father." The boy did not open his eyes.

"Well," said the Consul after a moment, "here we are, starting out again. It seems not a bad town. I hope you will like it."

"At least there is no garden."

"No," said the Consul heavily, as though that spared them both. "There is no garden."

A long pause followed. Would the boy never come back to him? Could he never forget these frightful weeks when Nicholas refused to look at him, but, lying motionless, with averted head, met his tenderest advances with the muttered though, of course, unmeant words: "I hate you."

Even when the shock of José's unfortunate passing had lost something of its sting, he had remained silent and apart, had spent much of his time with old Pedro and at the Burtons. Then, to Brande's secret dismay, he had begun to speak about his mother and to ask most distressing questions, requesting her photograph for his bedroom, pressing to know her address, and when he might see her again, wounding and embarrassing the Consul with even stronger demands.

Now, as at some inner prompting, the result of long well-guarded thought, he stirred, raised himself upon his elbow on the pillow.

"Father," he inquired, "where shall I have my lessons in this new town?"

"Why, my dear," Brande replied mildly, "I shall give them to you, as before."

"No, Father. I want to go to school."

Brande, despite himself, started slightly.

169

"But, Nicholas . . ."

"To school, Father . . . where I shall meet other boys, and play games . . . and perhaps make friends with them."

There was a pause.

"Well . . ." said the Consul in a subdued voice, "we shall see about it, my dear."

A short silence followed; then, as though nerving himself to speak, Nicholas gazed at the Consul and drew a quick, deep breath.

"There's something else, Father. I've . . . I've had a letter from Mother."

"What!"

The exclamation, torn it seemed from Brande's heart, made Nicholas blink a little, but he went on, a trifle unsteadily.

"You knew I had written to her, didn't you? What's more . . ." With a courageous rush, the words came out: "I wish to see her . . . soon, Father . . . as soon as possible. . . ."

Speechless under this unexpected bludgeoning, Brande stared at his son. Before he could recover himself, Nicholas rushed on:

"After all, she *is* my mother. . . . I have a right to be with her. And she has a right to be with me. There are ships which go from this port to America . . . large ships . . . we passed one as we came in to-day. And I am quite big now, able to travel by myself. . . ."

For an instant a surge of the old violent anger swelled in the Consul's breast like a serpent uncoiling itself to strike. But it was quickly over, lost in this new, this pitiful defencelessness—the certitude of his own vulnerability. He moistened his lips, at last found his tongue.

"Do you mean that she . . ."—he hesitated, almost gave way—"that she has asked you to . . . to stay with her?"

"Yes, Father."

"For how long?" He had to grope for the words.

From under the boy's lashes slipped an indefinable look, a mixture of sadness, triumph, and inflexible obstinacy.

"That depends on you, Father," he answered temperately, with unsuspected tact. "And on me, I suppose. But there is no doubt I should spend some time with Mother. That is only fair . . . to all of us."

In an access of distress, Brande pressed his hand to his brow, masking his eyes with trembling fingers, as though retreating from some crude hallucination. It was true, in a sense, that he had suspected an exchange of letters between Nicholas and his mother, had even, in a numb and distant fashion, envisaged the danger of their reunion. Yet the sudden presentation of the fact overwhelmed him. Dully, in a kind of daze, he asked himself how it had come about, how from that first unheeded moment twelve months before when he had engaged a simple Spanish lad to work his garden, this incredible result had sprung. Marion . . . his wife . . . resurrected from the dead and buried past . . . to share . . . perhaps even to steal the affections of his son.

It could not, must not be . . . no, no, he would never permit it. And yet, in the silent struggle which must now ensue, this gamble in which his sole remaining happiness was the stake, he could not infallibly foresee himself the victor.

"You do agree, don't you?" Nicholas was saying, in that same tone, persuasive, yet tempered by a new stringency. "You promise to make arrangements?"

Another pause. The Consul, still with bent head, striving to stiffen his will, made a blurred murmur which might have passed for either refusal or assent.

A long silence followed. Then, straightening, freeing himself from the phantoms of his meditation, swallowing down his pain, Brande laid his damp hand, entreatingly, on his son's arm.

"Nicholas," he said, with some return of his lofty manner, "many things have come between us in these past months. Although, God knows, my conscience is clear, if I have been in any way to blame, I am sorry. But don't let mere mischance . . . or unmeant mistakes . . . destroy our feeling for one another. We still have the future. If we try I am sure

171

one day we can recapture . . . these intimacies of heart and mind . . . which I prize above all else. . . ."

Again, at the end of that sad monologue, there was a lengthy silence, during which, against the dark back-drop of the uncurtained window, the lights of the aurora flashed and flickered—a flight of souls across the inscrutable sky. The Consul sighed heavily, rose to his feet in a half-hearted fashion, and was moving in resignation towards the door, when, at a thought, he stopped short, turned wistfully, though not with hope, towards the bed.

"You wouldn't . . ." As he spoke, in a low voice, he continued to watch his son with that sidelong anxious glance. "You wouldn't care for me . . . to read to you to-night?"

The boy withdrew his eyes. He was about to refuse, brusquely—the hard words had already formed on his lips. Then something overcame him. Abruptly he turned his head away.

"All right," he muttered. "If you wish."

A smile of gratification so strangely pathetic it was almost foolish spread over the Consul's distraught and haggard face. Clumsily, with undue haste, he went into the other room, rummaged in his valise, returned with the familiar red leather-bound volume. He cleared his throat.

"Let us take the chapter that deals with the characteristics of some of the larger Audubon birds—it's really most interesting . . . and instructive. Oh, it's so long since we had this little treat together."

Seating himself on the bed, he adjusted his spectacles, and in a suffused voice began to read:

"The turkey, a large domestic fowl, with a plumage which vies in splendour with the peacock, was in the first instance a native of the American continent, but has since been transported to many other lands. It is by nature a peculiar bird —assertive and self-sufficient—yet because of this inordinate vanity, liable to grave discomfitures . . ."

All at once he broke off.

Nicholas, turned sideways on the pillow, gazing with

172

eager eyes at the woman's photograph upon his bedside table, this strange yet sweet-faced woman who was his mother, who would soon take his head between her hands and press it to her breast, was not paying the least attention. He wasn't listening . . . no, not listening to him at all.

The Stars Look Down

by A. J. Cronin

This powerful masterpiece now available for the first time in paperback edition!

This book is about LIFE . . . ugly, beautiful, ironic, heroic, and despairing. It is a book about PEOPLE, the story of miners—their land, their lives, their loves, their fights and their scars. A book, deep in human sympathy, to stir the conscience of a nation.

The SUNDAY TIMES said—'His women are as brilliantly painted as his men. The wretched Jenny who pines for the genteel and comes to so miserable an end; the Laura who gives Joe his first big chance and permits herself to become his mistress; her sister whom the war so subtly changes, and the Sally whom a lesser novelist would have transformed into a second Gracie Fields—all of them are wonderfully good. It is a rich and rare panorama.'

THE NEW ENGLISH LIBRARY 7s. 6d.

The Citadel

by A. J. Cronin

One of the best loved novels of all time.
This is the story of a young, rough, idealistic doctor and his apprenticeship in life . . .
With his rare sympathy and unique understanding, A. J. Cronin creates in *The Citadel* a world so amazingly real that it remains in the mind long after the book is finished. This is the world of Dr. Andrew Manson, whom we first meet in his greenness, fresh from medical school, practising in the remote mining valleys of Wales. It is here that he makes fervent friends and avowed enemies . . . and discovers the men and women who are to dominate his existence.
Later the scene moves to London, where Andrew does well, too well . . . and becomes the slick, social doctor whom he so much used to despise. It takes the estrangement of his devoted young wife and all the efforts of those closest to him to bring him to his senses, and a renewed purpose.

THE NEW ENGLISH LIBRARY 5s.